Silhouetted by the Blue

Silhouetted by the Blue

WITHDRAWN

TRACI L. JONES

SQUARE
FISH

FARRAR STRAUS GIROUX
NEW YORK

SQUARE
FISH

An Imprint of Macmillan
175 Fifth Avenue
New York, NY 10010
mackids.com

Square Fish books may be purchased for business or promotional use.
For information on bulk purchases, please contact the Macmillan Corporate
and Premium Sales Department at (800) 221-7945 x5442 or by e-mail at
specialmarkets@macmillan.com.

Library of Congress Cataloging-in-Publication Data
Jones, Traci L.
    Silhouetted by the blue / Traci L. Jones.
        p. cm.
    Summary: After the death of her mother in an automobile accident, seventh-
grader Serena, who has gotten the lead in her middle school play, is left to handle
the day-to-day challenges of caring for herself and her younger brother when
their father cannot pull himself out of his depression.
    ISBN 978-1-250-05683-2 (paperback) / ISBN 978-1-4299-6253-7 (e-book)
    [1. Family problems—Fiction.   2. Depression, Mental—Fiction.   3. Grief—
Fiction.   4. Theater—Fiction.   5. Middle schools—Fiction.   6. Schools—
Fiction.   7. African Americans—Fiction.]   I. Title.

PZ7.J72752Si 2011
[Fic]—dc22   2010008419

Originally published in the United States by Farrar Straus Giroux
First Square Fish Edition: 2015
Book designed by Andrew Arnold
Square Fish logo designed by Filomena Tuosto

10 9 8 7 6 5 4

AR: 4.6 / LEXILE: 720L

For my husband, Tony, for loving me anyway . . .

and

*For my big brother, Peter C. Groff . . . I've named
a character after you, so you can now stop nagging me!
Love, your favorite, much-younger sister*

Children run so fast
Toward the future,
From the past . . .
Two small lives,
Silhouetted by the blue

—"Our Children," *Ragtime*

1

It wasn't clear to Serena Shaw which woke her
up—the burning smell or the persistent wail of the smoke
alarm. What *was* clear was that neither was a good sign.
Yanking back her covers, she rolled onto the floor and
crawled to the door. She felt a little silly creeping on the
floor like that, but her motto was "better safe than burnt
to a crisp." Serena tentatively placed a hand on the door.
It was stone cold. Getting to her feet, she pulled the door
open. She saw no sign of smoke, but there was definitely a
strong smell: burning bread. Serena clasped her hands
over her ears to muffle the wail of the alarm and bounded
into the hallway. In the dim light she saw that the door to
her father's room was closed, while the door to her brother's
room was wide open.

Oh, Henry, not again, she thought.

Serena stood outside her father's door for a moment,
waiting for him to come bursting out.

Maybe he's in the shower, she reasoned, *and has to dry off and pull on some pajama pants.* It was a sensible excuse for the lack of response, but deep down Serena knew it wasn't the truth.

Serena ignored the lump in the pit of her stomach and leaped down the stairs two at a time to the kitchen. She would check on her father later. Right now there was stuff to be done and she was the one who was going to have to do it.

In the kitchen, Serena placed her hands on her hips and looked around. A step stool was pushed up to the kitchen counter. An empty bagel bag lay open by an abundance of crumbs and a large knife. Smoke was pouring from the toaster where the poorly cut bagel was jammed into one of the slots. The too-thick slice was preventing the toaster from popping up and the bagel was getting darker and darker. *Henry, Henry, Henry,* Serena thought. Shaking her head, she unplugged the toaster and extracted the blackened bagel with a butter knife. Then she opened the back door and began fanning the smoke out of the kitchen with her social studies folder which she had left lying on the kitchen table the night before. After a few minutes the wailing of the smoke alarm stopped.

"Come on out, Henry," Serena finally said. "It's okay. No harm, no foul, no permanent lung damage."

Henry's face appeared from under the table.

"Sorry, sissy," he said, crawling out slowly. He wrapped his skinny arms around Serena's waist and looked up at her.

"Don't call me sissy," Serena said irritably, completely unmoved by his big brown-eyed, puppy-dog look. "And what were you thinking? You know you aren't supposed to use a sharp knife. And you cut it all wrong."

"Sorry," Henry repeated again, tears in his eyes. "I was hungry and I wanted a bagel."

"Why didn't you just wait for me?" Serena asked. She pulled his arms off her and pointed to the kitchen table, where he obediently sat down. From the refrigerator Serena pulled out the milk jug. It was almost empty. She sighed. They needed to go to the supermarket.

"You were taking too long, and Daddy said to get it myself," Henry explained, two fat tears rolling down his cheeks.

"Okay, okay, don't cry, it's not a big deal," Serena said. She glanced at the kitchen clock—7:35 a.m. "Oh, shoot, you don't have time for breakfast. Go get your shoes on."

"Daddy is supposed to walk me today," Henry whined. "He hasn't walked me for a whole week. I'm hungry. Can't I have a bagel?"

"You burned the last bagel, and Daddy's not going to walk you today. Come on! You'll be late."

Henry followed Serena out of the kitchen back upstairs. "You aren't even dressed. Why can't Daddy walk me? I'm gonna go ask him."

Serena pulled Henry away from their father's bedroom door. "I'll ask him. Just go get your shoes."

5

She waited until Henry reached his room before poking her head inside her father's door.

"Good morning, Dad," she said. "You getting up yet?"

"Good morning, sweetie," her father answered, without any energy in his voice. "Nah, I'm not feeling so great. I gotta rest. I gotta think." He rolled over to face the wall and pulled the covers up to his chin, curling into a ball.

Serena waited for a second, thinking that maybe, just maybe, he'd reconsider. When he didn't move she tried again.

"Daddy, Henry said you were supposed to take him to school today."

Nothing but silence came from the lump in the middle of his bed. Serena tried a different tack.

"Don't you have to finish those illustrations soon though?" she prodded, trying to use the same tone of voice her mother had used on her father. "For that elephant book? I thought you said it was due this week."

Her father shook his head slowly from side to side.

"Later, baby," he mumbled.

"But Henry—" Serena began again.

"Can you take him to school, please, Serena?"

"You feeling blue still, Daddy?" Serena whispered.

As an answer, her father rolled over again and pulled his pillow over his head.

"Okay, I'm guessing that's a yes then," Serena said softly.

Her father had always had cases of the blue from time to time. But her mother had always been around to deal with it—taking him to the doctor, making sure he got his medicine. And he always got better. It hadn't really had much of an impact on Serena's day-to-day life back then. But now that her mother was gone, Serena suddenly realized how serious the blue could really be.

"Hey, Dad, do you want me to get you a glass of water, so you can take your pill?" she said.

After a big sigh her father muttered, "I'm all out. Those pills make me sick to my stomach anyway. I'm not taking them anymore. Please. Just take Henry to school. Close the door on your way out."

Serena pulled the door shut and leaned up against it, willing the lump in her throat to dissolve. She missed her mother, too, a lot, but life just kept going on without her being alive. If Serena could force herself to keep moving, why couldn't her father? She was just a seventh grader. He was a grownup for God's sake. Clenching her fists, Serena pushed herself off the wall and shook those thoughts out of her head.

"I wish Mommy were here to walk me. Do you think her ghost had to stay in New Leans? Do they call it new 'cause they just built it?" Henry asked, coming out of his room.

"Mom is not a ghost in New Orleans. She's in heaven," Serena said, trying to stop the waves of annoyance that rushed over her. "And Daddy can't walk you because he's a little blue. Again." She tried to say all this in a kind voice, but she hated having this conversation with Henry every five minutes. When would he finally get it? Mom was gone. Dead. Had been for more than a year. Eighteen long, horrible months. It wasn't that hard a concept to get. Jeez.

"Oh, yeah, heaven. I forgot. Is it far? Can I go? She's been gone a long time, how come she left all of the sudden?" Henry asked, then burst out giggling. "You're silly, Daddy isn't blue, he's brown just like you. And I'm light brown just like Mommy is, except she's on a trip to heaven, right?"

Ignoring Henry's barrage of questions, Serena ducked into her room and grabbed a pair of jeans off the floor. She snatched a T-shirt out of her drawer and grabbed the nearest pair of tennis shoes. Henry was standing there watching her get dressed.

"Go get your stuff, Henry," Serena said, pushing him down the hallway to his room. She slipped into the bathroom and brushed her teeth, allowed herself a couple of tears, and then washed her face.

Henry reappeared in her room with his coat and his Spider-Man backpack, which he insisted on taking to school every day, even though Serena knew for a fact it contained nothing more than a bunch of his old drawings, some crayons, and maybe a broken pencil.

"Do you think that Spider-Man could fix the lean out for them?" asked Henry. "He's really strong. I bet he could just use a web to pull it straight and make it not lean."

It took Serena a minute to figure out what Henry was talking about, but she finally got it. "It's New *Or*leans, not New Leans," she said. She hoped that would satisfy Henry for a while. It was like he refused to accept the fact that their mom was *never* coming back from her business trip to New Orleans. He seemed to think that if he kept asking about her he might somehow get a different answer. Maybe it was just his way of dealing with things. Maybe they all had different ways of coping with her death. Serena had her singing. Henry had his questions, and the millions of pictures he drew. And her dad? Serena didn't know what he used to cope. Actually, she thought, he didn't seem to be coping at all.

"Okay, kiddo, let's break," Serena said. She grabbed a scrunchie and gathered up her braids into a ponytail and herded her little brother out of the door. On the days her father didn't walk him to school, Serena had to, which meant that she was always hurrying, especially if *she* was to get to school on time.

"Let me give Daddy a goodbye kiss first," Henry said. Serena rolled her eyes and followed him to their father's room.

Henry opened the door and bounded in. Her father had

9

emerged from under his pillow, but hadn't moved much otherwise.

"Bye, Daddy!" Henry yelled.

Serena leaned against the doorjamb and watched as her little brother hopped onto the bed and gave her father a big kiss on his cheek.

Her father patted him absentmindedly on the arm, but said nothing. Serena turned away. The least he could do was pull himself out of his little funk long enough to give his son a freaking goodbye kiss. What would it take? Like, five seconds of effort?

Henry had too much energy bouncing around his body to pay attention to anyone else. He came skipping out of the bedroom, slamming the door shut behind him, and reached for Serena's hand. Together they walked out the front door.

"Serena, what time does my school start?" Henry asked, swinging her arm wildly.

"Stop that!" Serena snapped. She held her arm as still as she could. "It starts at eight. Just like it did yesterday, and last month, and the month before that."

"What time does *your* school start, Serena?"

"Eight-fifteen."

Henry let go of her hand so he could grab a stick from the ground. "Is your school closer to our house or is mine?"

"Yours is a little closer, I guess," Serena answered.

Henry giggled as if that was the funniest joke ever.

"Ha!" he shouted, tossing the stick in the air in triumph. "I'm closer! I win!"

"It's not about winning, pinhead," Serena said. She ducked out of the way as the stick fell to the ground. "You are such a dimwit."

"No name-calling, or I'm telling," whined Henry. "I'm not a dimwit. You're a pumpkin face."

Serena swooped down and threw Henry over her shoulder like a sack of potatoes. He giggled, making his stomach bounce against her shoulder.

"You are a big ole bag of peanuts," she said, sliding Henry down lower. She turned her head and began blowing raspberries into her brother's warm neck. "A big old heavy sack of nuts."

Henry laughed, squirming around furiously. Serena hung on tightly until he plopped himself to the ground. The sudden weight off her shoulder was a relief, even though she missed the warmth of his body next to hers.

"You are a big ole bag of chocolate drops," he said, snatching her hand again.

"Chocolate drops?" Serena asked as they arrived at the elementary school. "I'm okay with being a chocolate drop. Okay, kid, go away, go learn something." She shooed him off into the schoolyard. "Hey, see if they're still serving breakfast, 'kay?"

Henry gave her a big hug and a soft kiss on the cheek.

"Bye, sissy, chocolate drop, pumpkin head girl," he said.

Henry gave her one last squeeze. "Love you." Then he ran off into the playground.

Serena watched him for a moment.

Yeah, I love you, too, pinhead, she thought to herself. Then she turned and headed toward her school.

2

Serena hurried to school more out of habit than out of any real desire to get there on time. Truth be told, she wouldn't much mind missing first-period math.

Just as Serena reached the crosswalk across from the school, the warning bell rang. She had five minutes to get her behind in her second-row, second-seat math chair. Her stomach growled. It would be just as easy to turn around and head a few blocks in the opposite direction to St. Mark's Bakery and Café and grab a bagel. Serena would bet the allowance that her father kept forgetting to give her that her best friends Nikka and Kat were there, ogling the local high school kids who were also skipping out on their first classes. Serena turned away from the light and looked longingly down the street in the direction of the coffeehouse.

Why bother going to class? she thought to herself. She had taken one step toward the coffeehouse when another thought leaped into her mind. Role assignments for the play came out today.

A shiver of excitement coursed through Serena's spine. There was nothing she wanted more than to get one of the lead roles in the school play. At last Friday's audition she'd changed the song she was going to sing at the last minute. She'd been planning to sing her mother's favorite song from *Ragtime*, "Our Children," but as she stood up there on the stage, just thinking about the lyrics made her eyes tear up. So instead she started singing a song from the play the school was putting on, *The Wiz*. It probably hadn't been a smart thing to do, but it had been the only song that popped into her head.

Serena punched the walk button until her finger hurt. If she did get a role in the play, she didn't want to blow her chances of keeping it by getting a bad grade in math. She was barely hanging on to a B– as it was. The light finally changed and Serena raced across the street, her backpack bumping against her leg as she ran. She reached her math class just as the final bell rang.

"Glad to see you could make it to class today, Miss Shaw," Mrs. Grayson said, shutting the door after Serena entered.

"What?" Serena protested, her voice all innocence and sweetness. "I've been in class every day this week!"

"It's Wednesday, Serena," Mrs. Grayson said. "Not that impressive a feat, I'd say."

Serena grinned. "Yeah, but it's a darn good start, right?"

Mrs. Grayson chuckled briefly before catching herself. "Sit down and get out your homework."

Serena sat down at her desk and made a flourish of pulling out her mostly completed homework. There were a few problems she hadn't finished, due to an important emergency phone call from Kat about her failing relationship with Charles. Besides, it wasn't like she would have been able to finish the homework anyway. Serena was terrible at math. Her mother had been the math whiz—the one who had always been around to help Serena with her homework. Her father was useless with math . . . and with just about everything else, too, Serena thought bitterly. At least lately.

Besides, school didn't float Serena's boat. She didn't care about geometry or geography. Serena wanted to sing. She wanted to act. Knowing when the Civil War ended or how to solve a quadratic equation wouldn't get her into Juilliard. And ever since her mother had died she had even less of a reason to keep her grades up. Last report card, her father hadn't said a thing when a couple of her C's slipped to D's. If it weren't for the tryouts for the spring musical, she'd probably have a few F's. But if you were flunking out you couldn't be in the play, and then what would they show when they did a retrospective of your life during the Tony Awards?

When choir rolled around, Serena hurried to her locker.

She could feel the excitement course up and down her spine like an electric eel. She knew that the cast list would be posted on the choir room door. She desperately wanted to be Dorothy, the lead, but the most coveted roles usually went to eighth graders—even though everyone knew that all the strongest singers were in her class.

Serena opened her locker and stowed her coat and backpack. One of the best things about choir was that all you needed was conveniently located right there in your body. No annoying books to drag around.

"Hey, Serena," said a voice behind her.

Serena sighed. "Hey, Candy," she said, turning with a smile. It was Candice Rudolph, otherwise known as Candy, and one of the best singers in the seventh grade, along with Serena.

It was entirely possible that Candy had gotten the lead. She could perform it as well as Serena could. That was the truth and Serena knew it, which proved that sometimes the truth not only hurts, but also bites the big one. Serena wished she could dislike Candy, just a little. It would make life a lot easier. Unfortunately, Candy was just like her name, sweet and likable. Plus, she was so freaking cute with those light brown eyes and that good hair.

"You ready to look?" Candy asked, hooking her arm around Serena's and pulling her down the hall. "I just know you got the lead! Your audition was off the chain!"

"Yeah, I guess," Serena answered back. Her electric eel turned into a stomach full of nervous butterflies. "I don't know though, I mean, we're only in seventh. And you were real good, too."

Candy waved a dismissive hand. "I should have done a song like you did, one from the play. It really showed off your voice and your range. I could totally picture you singing it on opening night. It was like, 'Hey, y'all! You're looking at Dorothy!'"

"Yeah, well, you did great with that Whitney Houston song," Serena answered. "I can't even reach some of the notes you can get up to!"

They both stopped short as they came to the crowd around the choir door.

"Good luck," Candy said, pulling a suddenly reluctant Serena close toward the cast list.

"You, too," Serena said, although she wasn't sure she meant it.

"Oh, my God!" squeaked Candy delightedly.

Serena's heart sank at Candy's excitement. So she hadn't gotten Dorothy after all. She couldn't bring herself to look at the list.

"Oh, Serena, you're so silly. Look up at the list, girl!"

Serena raised her head slowly, steeling herself to

congratulate Candy politely. Then she looked at the first two lines and stopped reading—and breathing.

THE WIZ CAST LIST

Dorothy . . . . Serena Shaw

Addaperle / Auntie Em / Dorothy
   Understudy . . . . Candice Rudolph

"Oh, my God!" Serena shouted. "I don't believe it!"

"Well, believe it," said Mr. Hobbs, poking his head around the choir room door. "Now get in class, we'll talk about the play after school."

Both girls floated happily into the room, parting as Candy went to the soprano section and Serena to the altos.

All through class, Serena could barely sing properly. Forming the words in their songs proved difficult with such a wide grin.

When class was over, Mr. Hobbs called Serena and Candy aside.

"I wanted to congratulate you both on your roles," he told them. "I have to say, it was tough for me to choose who to cast as Dorothy, but I do think that the Dorothy songs are suited for a voice in the lower registers. That really was the deciding factor. You both were fabulous at tryouts."

"Oh, Serena is *so* the perfect choice, Mr. Hobbs," said Candy with a sincere smile and a squeeze of Serena's hand. "I am honored to even be her understudy. I can't wait to get started!"

"Wonderful. I'll need you two in the auditorium immediately after eighth period," he said.

"We'll be there!" Candy chirped for the both of them.

But the smile on Serena's face faded.

"Is there a problem?" Mr. Hobbs asked.

"Oh, no, sir," said Serena, plastering a big, fake smile on her face again.

"Oh, okay," said Mr. Hobbs, relieved. "Don't be nervous, Serena. You'll be great. You both will."

"Well, we better go to third!" Candy said. "See ya after school."

Serena hurried to her locker to grab her Spanish books, all the while thinking about rehearsal after school. How was she supposed to get there right after eighth period and pick Henry up, too? Under normal, unblue, circumstances, her father would pick Henry up and walk him home. Or on the days when he had a presentation, her mother would have left early from work to get him. But today, well, her father wasn't very likely to even get out of bed, much less leave the house. Maybe she should call her father at lunch to see if he was feeling well enough to pick up Henry. Maybe he'd just been having a bad morning. Maybe his blue would go away quicker than it ever had before. Maybe, maybe, maybe. Serena slammed her locker door shut. She *hated* maybes.

3

Serena rushed to her Spanish desk and pulled out her homework, which had been another unfortunate victim of the Kat/Charles drama. Miss Capra was busy writing on the board, so Serena tried to finish as quickly as she could, which, given her pitiful Spanish skills, wasn't very fast.

"Dang, Serena, again?" a voice whispered.

Serena looked up from her furious writing. Elijah Mills had twisted around in his seat and was smirking at her.

Serena grinned at him. "What can I say?" she whispered. Miss Capra was still writing on the board. "I love to live on the edge. I bet I've got at least another forty-five, fifty seconds to finish." Serena went back to her homework, but she couldn't focus properly. She couldn't help wondering when Elijah had gotten so cute.

"Yeah, okay," Elijah said with a chuckle. "Here."

He pulled out his perfect homework paper and slid it onto her desk.

"Oh, thanks!" Serena said, copying the rest of her homework from him.

"No worries."

"*Clase, por favor, pasen sus papeles al frente,*" announced Miss Capra, turning around from the board just as Serena finished copying the last problem.

Serena passed their homework to Elijah and winked at him.

"*Gracias,* I owe you!" she whispered.

Elijah winked back. "*No hay problema. Para alguien tan hermosa y especial como tu, haría cualquier cosa.*"

Serena frowned. "Huh? Doesn't '*hermosa*' mean brother or something?"

"*Señorita Shaw!*" Miss Capra snapped. "*Por favor deje de hablar y preste atención.*"

"Huh?" Serena repeated. Miss Capra frowned at her. Serena slunk down in her seat. She hated Spanish.

Finally, after an eternity, Spanish ended and Serena hurried back to her locker to grab her purse for lunch. Her girls, Kat and Nikka, were already there and they had their jackets on. Serena could immediately tell by all their primping that staying in the school was out. Nikka was busy pulling her twists into a ponytail so she wagged her elbow at Serena by way of a greeting. Kat was glossing her lips.

"Hey, girlie," offered Kat, giving her a one-armed squeeze. "Want to sneak off campus with us and take a long lunch at St. Mark's? Check out the high school honeys?"

"I can't," Serena said. She had to run to the office to call her father about Henry.

"Oh, come on!" Nikka snapped, sounding annoyed as usual. "We'll be back by sixth period, seventh, no later. Don't be such a buzzkill."

"Love to, but can't," Serena told her. "Maybe another day. Why don't you guys just head to the caf and I'll meet you there? Let's do St. Mark's tomorrow instead."

"Nah, we're not feeling the caf today," Kat answered, shaking her head.

"Well, don't take all the cuties. Leave some for me," Serena replied. "I'll distract Mr. Childs for you. 'Cause I'm cool like that."

"That's the least you can do since you're buggin' out on us," Nikka said.

"Yeah, whatever," Serena snapped. "You're welcome."

Kat and Nikka walked a little ahead of Serena, slowly passing by Mr. Childs, the elderly security guard, who was standing directly in front of the doors to make sure there were no escapees. Serena came up right behind him.

"Oh, Mr. Childs?" she said, her voice full of innocence.

"Yes," the old man said, turning away from the doors.

"Well, um, I, well, you know," Serena stammered, as if she was unsure of what she was going to say next. She bit her lip, widened her eyes, and looked at the security guard with embarrassment and concern. Then she motioned for him to step away from the doors as though she wanted to tell him something without anyone else hearing. "I don't like being a tattletale."

"Now, don't you worry about that," Mr. Childs said, patting her on the arm. While he spoke, Kat and Nikka eased open the front doors and slipped outside. Through the large windows, Serena could see them running toward the street.

"Well," Serena continued, "um, I just came out of the girls' bathroom upstairs by the library, and I *know* I smelled cigarette smoke in the stall next to me." She rearranged her face to show concern mixed with a dash of virtuous indignation.

"Thank you for reporting it," Mr. Childs said seriously. "Don't you worry one bit. You are not being a tattletale. You are simply reporting something that needs to be reported. You're a good girl."

Serena conjured up a Candy-like smile. "Thank you," she said sweetly. "I feel much better now. Have a good day, sir."

Mr. Childs gave a brief glance out of the front door and, seeing nothing afoul, hurried off to investigate the illicit smoking in the girls' second-floor bathroom.

Serena was actually glad to have a valid excuse to blow off Kat and Nikka. It was one thing to ditch a class here and there or sneak off campus for lunch once or twice a

23

month, but with those two it was becoming a weekly thing. How they got away with it Serena didn't understand. Besides, it took all the fun out of it when you did it too regularly.

She had just reached the office when it dawned on her that she didn't have to worry about picking up Henry today. He had a playdate. Still, she wanted to call her father and tell him the good news about the role in the play. Unfortunately, someone else had beaten her to the phone, so she would have to wait. It was Myron Thomas, the biggest whining, namby-pamby crybaby in the seventh grade. Serena figured that's what his parents got for naming their kid Myron.

"But, Mom," Myron whined into the phone. "I told you specifically last night that I did not want bologna today. I wanted a simple peanut butter sandwich. I need the extra protein to get through my last classes of the day. I need you to bring me a new lunch."

"Oh, you have got to be kidding me," Serena muttered. She heaved a dramatic sigh and leaned on the office counter, drumming her fingers.

Myron turned and glared at her. Covering the mouthpiece of the phone, he said, "I'll thank you to keep your ears out of my conversation, Miss Serena Shaw."

"Well, then you'll have to whine more quietly, Myron," Serena answered back.

Myron huffed at Serena and cupped his hand over his

24

mouth. "Yes, well, you have to hurry," he whispered. "I've wasted at least six minutes of my lunch period with this mistake. *No, no!* Not that kind. Yes, the all-natural peanut butter. No, I keep it in *my* cabinet. Yes, right next to the whey powder. In fact, give the peanut butter a little sprinkle of whey before you slice it. Yes, Mother, hurry. You know I don't like to eat quickly. It messes with my digestive system. I prefer my lunch to be at least halfway digested by the middle of sixth period. You see the bathroom is halfway . . ."

"Oh, lawd!" Serena moaned. "Would someone please shoot you and put you out of *my* misery?"

The school secretary snorted with laughter, but quickly covered it up with a fake cough. Myron glared at Serena again.

"Mother, I'll be waiting at the front door. I have to go now. Other, ruder students are waiting to use this phone. If you would buy me that cell phone I've been asking for, I could have texted you before school started and gotten this resolved much sooner. Yes, we *will* be discussing it tonight. See you soon, I hope." Myron returned the phone to the receiver and shot Serena a final glare on his way out.

The workers in the office waited half a second after Myron had left before bursting out with laughter. Serena would have joined in, but she was too nervous about her phone call to her father.

As she dialed, the lack of privacy made her wish Myron's mother had bought her a cell phone, too.

One, two, three, four, five times the phone rang. Serena knew that the answering machine would pick up soon. On the sixth ring her father picked up.

"Yeah?" he said. A corpse would have had a livelier voice than her father's.

"I got the lead, Daddy!" Serena told her father excitedly. "I'm Dorothy in *The Wiz!*" Her announcement was met by a long silence.

"I have a meeting after school," Serena continued. "But don't worry about picking Henry up. He's got that play-date with Malik."

Her father said nothing.

Serena waited. Finally, her father spoke.

"Okay," he said. "Bye." And he hung up.

Serena held the phone to her ear, the smile disappearing from her face like the sun behind a rain cloud.

"Bye, Daddy," she said softly to the dial tone.

Serena stood for a moment, looking at the phone, imagining a different conversation in her head.

"Hey, Daddy, guess what?" she would say. "I got the lead in the school play!"

"Oh that's wonderful, baby girl," he'd gush back. "I'll be front row at every performance! Your mother would have been so proud of you. Hurry home tonight so we can all go out for dinner to celebrate!"

"Are you done with the phone or what?" a voice behind her said, startling Serena out of her daydream.

"Oh, yeah, sorry," Serena said. She gathered her things and headed to the cafeteria.

Sliding her tray down the line, Serena shook off her sadness and turned her thoughts to the play. Today they'd get their playbooks and meet each other. She couldn't wait! Exiting the line with her carton of orange juice, fries, and a cup of chocolate pudding, Serena stood at the front of the lunchroom and considered her options.

Since Kat and Nikka had abandoned her, their usual table was empty. She spotted Myron sitting with his friend, still waiting for his whey and peanut butter sandwich, but she definitely wasn't sitting there. Shifting her tray to her hip, she spotted Candy and her best friend Desiree and was starting to head in their direction when she suddenly spotted Elijah.

"*Hola, amigo!*" she said, plopping her tray down on his table. Since he was at the edge of the bench she had to sit extremely close to him.

"*Aqui está mi persona favorita,*" Elijah said with a smile.

"Scoot over, dude, give a lady some room," Serena answered, bumping him with her hip. *Did he just say "favorite person"?* she wondered. Maybe he was just trying to butter her up so she'd let him meet her dad. Elijah was one of the best artists in school, and he'd often told her how much he loved her father's book illustrations.

27

"Siempre puedes sentarse al lado de mí," he answered with a smirk.

"Did you say *'sentarse'* or *'sentirse'*?" Serena asked. "And why do you speak Spanish so freakin' well? Why are you in Spanish 1B instead of, like, Spanish for geniuses or something?"

"Well, some of us are just smarter than others, I guess," Elijah said.

"Oh, la-di-da," Serena said. She shoved a fry in her mouth. "And some of us are more arrogant and self-centered."

"Don't be a hater," Elijah admonished. "Or all homework assistance will disappear."

"Oh! Okay, then!" Serena said. "You are my Spanish idol! You the man, I mean *hombre*."

"Nah, for real, though," Elijah said with a grin. "My nanny back in the day spoke only Spanish, and I guess I picked it up after eight or nine years of hearing it all the time. I didn't think I remembered it till class, then it all just sort of came back. I skipped Spanish 1A last semester if that makes you feel any better. Anyway, I understand we are all supposed to be congratulating you and stuff."

"Huh?" Serena said, finishing her fries.

"Yeah, right. I guess that's supposed to be your version of modesty? The big star of the play pretending not to know what her lowly classmate is talking about?"

Serena finally caught on. "Ohh, yeah, thank you, thank you, thank you!" She bowed to Elijah and then to her orange juice.

"Thank you, thank you!" Elijah mimicked. "Um, now who's being all arrogant and stuff?"

"What? Are you making fun of me?" Serena poked him with the end of her plastic spoon.

Elijah held his hand to his heart. "I would *never* insult you, Serena. *You* are like my favorite person ever."

"Okay, whatever, Mr. Funnyman. Hey!" Serena said, suddenly having an idea. She poked him with her spoon again. "You should be on the scenery crew for the play! You are like the bomb artist!"

Elijah finished chewing his bite of apple before answering.

"The play? Drama club?" He shook his head. "Nah, I don't think so. I'm much too cool for that."

"Oh, you gotta do it, Elijah!" Serena said, jabbing him with her spoon again. "As the star of the play, I think the rules are that I get whatever I want."

"Okay," Elijah said. "First of all, you need to stop beating me up with eating utensils, and second, congratulations, and *finalmente, si significa que voy a verte mas, entonces definitivamente lo haría*."

"You know what?" Serena said. "You keep speaking Spanish to me I'm going to go get a fork. Please, please,

Elijah, you're the best artist in the school. I've peeped all your drawings at the art show the last few years. Besides, you aren't all that cool anyway."

"Ah, so you've checked out my stuff, have you?" Elijah said, stroking his chin and nodding. "Well, when you put it like that, then sure. For you, my love, anything. And, I'll just ignore that last comment."

Serena raised her eyebrows. Elijah had become such a flirt lately that she didn't know when to take him seriously. "Honest? You will?"

Elijah leaned over and whispered into her ear. "*Sí, como no?*"

Serena grabbed the plastic fork off of Elijah's tray and jabbed him in the leg.

4

The rest of the day, Serena had a hard time concentrating. With the *Wiz* meeting to look forward to, time dragged by slowly, and her ability to pay attention to what her teachers were saying was nil.

Finally, *finally*, the last bell rang. Serena felt like skipping, but as she turned the corner to the auditorium she spotted Elijah and a couple of his friends leaning against the wall.

"I was thinking you might dog me out and not show up!" Serena called to him.

"Nah, word is bond," he answered.

He was looking at her so intensely that it made her a little nervous. She looked down at her shirt, trying to find a ketchup or pudding stain.

"What, I got a spot or something?" she asked.

Elijah tilted his head. After a moment he said, "Nah, I'm just trying to see if you look like a star."

Serena flicked him on the arm. "Boy, you had me all nervous!"

"*Te podria mirar todo el día,*" Elijah said, holding the door to the auditorium open for her with a flourish.

Serena pointed her finger at him. "Look, don't you even start with the Spanish stuff, or I swear I will go get a plastic eating utensil and gut you with it."

"Well, you may not *be* a real star yet, but you are sure acting like one," Elijah said, bowing to her as she sauntered past him into the auditorium.

Elijah took a seat a few rows back, but Mr. Hobbs waved Serena down to the front where Candy and several of the other principal cast members were sitting.

"Thank you all for coming so promptly," Mr. Hobbs shouted over the chattering and excited conversations. The students quickly became quiet. "I'm very pleased with the turnout, especially for chorus and stagehands. I think this year's musical will be a great success. Actually, it has to be. We've got a very special situation this year and I'll need everyone's pledge that they will work hard. I don't know how many of you follow the local news, but our school district is in a severe budget crunch. Programs and funding are being slashed left and right, and unfortunately the drama program here at Grove is one of those slated to be eliminated."

Serena gasped. And she wasn't the only one.

"Now, don't panic yet," Mr. Hobbs said. "We've been

granted a unique opportunity to save our program." He paused. Serena and the rest of the students looked at him. He took a breath and continued. "The Eugene Arts Foundation has generously offered our drama department a grant for $50,000. However, the grant is contingent on this year's performance. Unless we wow them—and we must—the committee will not give us the money. If any of you saw last year's performance of *Fiddler on the Roof*, you probably noticed that some of the lead actors failed to commit the script and the lyrics to memory. We cannot have a repeat of that fiasco. If we do, we will lose the chance to save ourselves."

Last year's play had been pretty awful. Serena had been in the chorus and had tried to get her father *not* to go.

"If Grove did receive the grant money," Mr. Hobbs continued, "it would mean the drama department would be safe for three years. Maybe four, with my penny-pinching skills. We could do a play, a musical, *and* a mime show." A spat of tittering rippled through the auditorium. "Oh, fine," Mr. Hobbs said. "Not a mime show. The important part is that the deadline to apply for the grant money is only seven weeks away. So instead of the twelve weeks of rehearsal we normally have, we'll need to attain perfection in a little more than half that time. The committee will be here on opening night."

Serena sucked in her breath. Would they really be able to pull everything together so quickly?

Mr. Hobbs went on. "Everyone who has a major speaking part in this production has an understudy. If you miss five rehearsals, whether excused absences or not, you will be replaced. If you are tardy to five rehearsals, you will be replaced. If you are not off book three weeks before opening night, you will be replaced. If you do not know the lyrics to all the songs you are performing by two weeks before opening night, you will be replaced. If you do not have the dance sequences down perfectly one week before opening night, you will be replaced. You are all old enough to understand responsibility. I expect each and every one of you to take your role in this production seriously. I expect each and every one of you to be responsible not only to yourself and your commitment but also to your fellow cast members. However, despite the fact that this production is very important to all of us, school is even more important. Do not even think about using your participation in the play as an excuse not to do homework, or to fail to turn in assignments in a timely manner. Participation in this production is not a 'get out of class free' pass. This afternoon, I gave a list of every cast member to every teacher at Grove. They will be giving me weekly reports on each of your grades. If any one of you, whether it's a munchkin or Dorothy herself, if *anyone's* grade point average falls below 2.75, you will be replaced. No exceptions." Mr. Hobbs paused here for a brief second and Serena thought he glanced down at her. Her face went hot.

"That's not only me talking," Mr. Hobbs continued, "but it's also the requirement for the grant money. If there is anyone who thinks they cannot live up to those rules, please leave now."

A couple of people sitting in the back scurried out of the auditorium. Mr. Hobbs watched them go and then made notations on a clipboard. Serena stayed seated, but she couldn't help feeling nervous. The last time she checked, her grade point average was only 2.85, and even she had to admit that was cutting it pretty close. Her stomach clenched in anxiety.

"Fine, now that we've separated the wheat from the chaff, it is time for script distribution. As is theater tradition, the first script goes to our lead, Miss Serena Shaw." Mr. Hobbs pulled a brand-new script off the pile and handed it to Serena with a flourish. "Our star. Our Dorothy. I'm sure she will lead us all to a fabulous show. As is also our tradition, started right after the district started cutting my funds, she will also be our assistant director."

Much to Serena's surprise the auditorium erupted into applause and cheers. She gave a sheepish grin and a brief wave to her fellow castmates. She should have been thrilled. Instead, Serena was totally stressed. As she riffled through the script, she realized that she was in every single scene.

And she sang more than half the songs. How on earth was she going to learn all those lines and the lyrics and the dances? Not to mention keep her grades up? Who would watch Henry while she was at rehearsals?

"Isn't that right, Dorothy?" asked Mr. Hobbs with a nod.

Serena looked up from her script to find everyone staring at her. "Um, I'm sorry, Mr. Hobbs, but . . ."

Mr. Hobbs clapped his hands in delight. "Look at that, folks! What an inspiration! Our star is trying to learn her script already! If we all follow Serena's wonderful example we will wow the Eugene Arts Foundation for certain. Okay, people, let's divide up! All nonspeaking munchkins to the choir room! Tornado dancers to the dance room! All speaking parts please head to the back of the room and start running your lines. Let's see now, is there an Elijah Mills here?"

"Yo!" Elijah shouted from the back of the auditorium.

"Yes, yo to you as well," Mr. Hobbs shouted back. "Please come down front. I have it from our esteemed art teacher that you are hands down the best artist here at Grove. I need to discuss with you what our scenery needs will be. Mrs. Giadono told me that you are more than capable of leading the project, so unless you have objections, you are now officially our set director."

Serena looked at Elijah's stunned face and couldn't help chuckling.

"I told you that you were the man," she said as she slipped past him on her way to join the other leads.

"Oh, you *so* owe me, *mi pájaro hermoso*," Elijah told her over his shoulder as he hurried down to talk with Mr. Hobbs.

Laughing, Serena joined Candy and the rest of the people with speaking roles. She plopped down in a seat and flipped to the first page of the script. All was quiet for a few minutes. When she looked up she again found that everyone was watching her, waiting.

"Oh, sorry, y'all," Serena said nervously. She supposed as the assistant director she needed to take charge. "Um, let's do a read-through first. As Maria Von Trapp would say, 'Let's start at the very beginning.' Act one, scene one."

Two hours later, Mr. Hobbs let them go. Serena walked out into the dimming afternoon light. Candy caught up with her, and together they waited for the light, talking excitedly about how the first rehearsal had gone.

"You were great today, Serena," Candy gushed. "After seeing all the stuff you have to do, and all the lyrics and lines you have, I gotta say I'm so happy I didn't get Dorothy after all. Plus, you play her perfectly. You seem all sad and lost, just like Dorothy should be. This play is going to be hot!"

"I seem sad?" Serena asked.

"Yeah, girl, you know, melancholy. Especially that first scene when you ask if I, I mean Auntie Em, you know, when you ask me if I would be happy if you'd suddenly disappear, right before the song 'The Feeling We Once Had'?"

"Hmmm," Serena responded with a nod. As Candy launched into a one-sided discussion of the play, Serena's mind started to drift away from school, to her house, right up the stairs and into her father's bedroom. She wondered whether he had picked up Henry from his playdate. It was getting pretty late. Mom had never wanted Henry to spend hours and hours at Malik's house. But what Mom wanted and what she had done didn't matter anymore. Sometimes it felt like just yesterday she had died, and sometimes it felt like an eternity. In two weeks and two days it would be exactly eighteen months to the day. Before her mind could go over that horrible thought again, like a tongue going to the hole in your mouth from a lost tooth, Serena forced herself to listen to Candy.

". . . like you. I was a mess for months and months," Candy finished softly.

"Huh?" Serena said. She had no clue what Candy was talking about.

"When my mom died," Candy said quietly, shooting Serena a quick glance. "I cried all the time and barely talked to anyone for months. Remember? You are so much stronger than I ever was."

Serena felt a lump appear in her throat. She had totally forgotten that Candy's mother had died, too. She didn't say anything for a minute, until she felt she could talk around the lump without her voice quivering.

"You were pretty young," she finally said. "When was it? Like third grade? Henry's in second grade and he barely even gets it. He keeps asking when Mom's . . ."

Serena stopped talking. She shoved her hands into her pockets and clenched her fists until her nails dug into the soft flesh of her palms. If she concentrated on the pain in her hands she could blink away her tears without any of them spilling over.

"Well, anyway," Serena continued finally, "there's nothing you can do about it, you know. You just gotta keep going."

"Yeah, it sucks, though," Candy answered. "The worst was that no one ever wanted to talk about it. Half my friends stopped talking to me altogether and the other half treated me like some sort of freak. Like my mother dying was contagious. Every time I even mentioned my mom, someone would immediately change the subject. I finally just gave up."

Serena nodded, still not trusting her voice.

"What I'm trying to say is that if you ever want to talk about your mom, or if you ever need something, let me know, 'kay? Of course, you probably do that with Kat and Nikka already, but I just wanted to say that I'm, you know, around. Well, I'm this way. Catch you later, Doro-thy!"

"Yeah, thanks, Candy," Serena said with a small smile. "I mean, Auntie Em!"

She stood at the corner, watching Candy walk away. Serena had always thought of herself as one of the cool kids, like Kat and Nikka. Totally different from Candy, who struck Serena as a little old-fashioned—sweet, but definitely not up-to-date. Maybe that was because she'd been living with her grandmother ever since her mother died. Now, though, Serena was starting to think that maybe hanging out with Candy for the next seven weeks might be a nice break from her usual crew. It wasn't that Serena's friends weren't great, but sometimes they acted exactly like Candy had described—if Serena even men-tioned her mom they got all weird and silent. She had got-ten used to acting like nothing was different whenever she was with them. But maybe she should give Candy more of a chance.

Serena hummed a little of the first song that Dorothy sang and grinned to herself. Dorothy didn't have a mom either, so Serena *was* perfect for the part.

After a few seconds though, Serena's smile faded and she stopped humming. It occurred to her that her father probably hadn't left his bedroom at all today. Serena sighed and headed toward Malik's house.

5

Serena shuffled impatiently in the doorway as Malik's mother searched for the boys. After a few minutes of looking she finally found them hiding in the basement. Serena frowned at Henry as he slumped to the front door.

"Say thank you to Henry for coming over, Malik," his mother said.

Malik stuck his tongue out at them before running off.

"Boy, come back here and say thank you!" his mother called after him.

Henry started to giggle, but Serena frowned at him again. He slapped a hand over his mouth but continued to laugh.

"Malik, come back here now and say goodbye to your friend!" his mother called lamely. She turned to Serena and sighed. "He's just too much. That's why we only have the one."

You only NEED the one! Serena thought. She poked Henry.

"Thank you for having me over, Mrs. Jackson," he said on cue.

"Oh, sweetie, you can come over anytime," Mrs. Jackson gushed. "You are such a good influence on Malik. You two may not have had your mom for long, but she sure did a great job with you while she was here."

Serena took a deep breath. It was definitely time to go. She turned and reached for the door, but was interrupted by Henry.

"Mommy's in heaven and Daddy's got the blue," he chirped.

"Yes, she is, bless her poor sainted soul. And I didn't know your father had the flu," said Malik's mother. "You be careful not to get it yourself."

"Yes, ma'am, we will," Serena said, taking a step out the front door. She grabbed Henry by the hood of his coat and started to tow him out after her.

"No, not flu!" Henry said. "The blue! It won't let Daddy get out of bed."

"My, he must have a really bad case." Mrs. Jackson looked concerned. "Should I come by? Bring him some soup, or you two some dinner?"

"No!" Serena told her quickly. "It's nothing. He's just a little under the weather, that's all."

Malik's mother nodded knowingly. "Well, just make

42

sure he has plenty of fluids, and I'm sure he'll be fine in a few days."

"Yes, ma'am. Plenty of fluids. Bye!"

When Malik's front door finally closed, Serena rounded on Henry in a fury. "Boy! You need to learn how to keep your big mouth shut!" she shouted at him. "What happens at home is nobody's business. You understand me? Don't you ever tell anyone! Got it? Nobody!"

Henry looked up at her, his big brown eyes filling with tears. "I'm sorry, Serena," he said. "I'm sorry, don't be mad at me. Don't go away. Don't leave me."

"I'm not going anywhere," Serena snapped. "Every time I yell at you, you say that, and every time I tell you the same thing!" She walked off quickly, making Henry trot to keep up. Every now and then she heard him sniff.

After a block or so Serena slowed and looked down at him. He had stopped crying, but his nose was runny, and she could see the white salty streaks of dried tears on his soft brown cheeks. She stopped walking and pulled him into a big hug.

"I'm sorry I yelled at you, stinky," she said softly. She knelt down so she could talk with him face-to-face. "It's just that not everyone can understand the blue. Some people might think that Daddy's just being lazy or something. They wouldn't understand how sad and tired the blue makes him. So for now, let's just keep it a secret between me, you, and Daddy. Okay?" *And if someone knew then*

43

maybe they'd take him away, she thought. *And then what would we do?* If their father got sent somewhere to get well, where would she and Henry go? Serena had seen an old movie where they'd carted someone off to the nuthouse. She couldn't let that happen to their dad. Maybe she was overreacting, but telling someone about Dad wasn't a chance she wanted to take.

She looked carefully at Henry, who hadn't said a word. At last he said, "Mommy's in heaven now because I made her mad and that made her leave."

"What?" Serena asked.

"It's my fault Mommy is gone. She was mad at me and then she left and then she didn't come back and now she's in heaven." Henry's eyes filled with tears again. "I'm sorry I made her go away, Serena. I'm real sorry. I didn't mean to."

"Henry," Serena started. She pulled him close. "It's not your fault that Mommy's in heaven. It was a car accident, remember?"

Henry shook his head furiously. "Mommy told me to clean my room and not put anything under the bed, but I did it anyway and then she found all my toys under there. And she was real mad. Then she left and didn't come back."

"Henry, Mom left because she had to give a marketing presentation in New Orleans. She was in the rental car and a big truck came and hit her and hurt her real bad."

44

The lump in Serena's throat appeared again. She swallowed a couple of times before continuing. "Remember, she called from the hospital and talked to us?" Henry nodded, and she pulled him into a tight hug. "Then the next day, when she was supposed to call and tell us good morning, the doctor in New Orleans called instead to tell us that the accident had caused a blood clot and Mom had died and gone up to heaven. Remember, Henry? It wasn't your fault. It wasn't anyone's fault but the stupid truck driver's, and that dumb blood clot's, I promise. I'd tell you if I thought it was your fault. Okay? I wouldn't lie about that. Not ever."

Henry took a long, snorting sniff and nodded. "Malik told me it was all my fault 'cause when we were supposed to be cleaning up the mess we made in his room his mom came in and told him he'd better get it done or she'd leave him and run off with the circus. And he laughed at me when I started cleaning, but I told him about Mommy and he told me it was all my fault."

"Both Malik and his momma are stupid," Serena snapped, thankful for the sudden rush of irritation that was helping to dry her tears.

"Ooooh!" Henry said, pointing an accusing finger right in Serena's face. "That's a bad word! My teacher says!"

"No it's not, it's a good word that describes Malik perfectly."

"No, sir," Henry said, and he launched into a detailed

lecture of why the word was bad. Serena started walking again, relieved that her brother's tears were already forgotten.

"So, tell me," Serena said, once Henry had finally stopped his yammering. "What do you want for dinner? Macaroni and cheese or hot dogs?"

"Macaroni and cheese! Can I help cook dinner tonight?" Henry asked, swinging Serena's arm back and forth wildly.

"Do you have to do that every time we walk? It's so annoying. I've told you that like a million times. And yes, you can help make dinner, unless you have homework."

"I've already done my whole homework packet already," Henry declared proudly.

"Jeez, you are such a geek. Well, *I* have lots of homework, and I need to get at least scene one of the play memorized. Hey! Henry, guess what? I'm Dorothy!"

Henry cracked up. "That's a big ole fat hairy lie. You're not Dorothy! You're Serena."

Serena rolled her eyes at her little brother.

"No, pinhead, there's going to be a play at school called *The Wiz*, and in the play I get to be Dorothy. I get to sing and dance and act."

"*You* get to be on television?" Henry looked up at her in awe.

"No, but I get to be onstage with a big spotlight on me!" Serena said proudly.

46

"Whoa, you must be pretty important," Henry said. "Or famous."

"I am. I am the star of the play. I'm on the stage in every scene." She was happy to finally get an excited reaction from someone she loved.

"Yeah, we're going to be rich!" Henry shouted. "I want a pool right in our basement!"

"Boy, we aren't going to be rich." Serena rolled her eyes again. "It's just a middle school play."

Henry pouted. "But you said you were going to be a star."

"I am, but I don't get any money for it. But if I'm really good the school will!"

"Oh." Henry was clearly no longer interested. "Serena, are we dolphins?"

"What are you talking about? We're people, you little nimrod," she answered. Sometimes talking with Henry was tiring.

"Malik said I was a dolphin because Mommy died," Henry said.

Serena stopped walking.

"What did that boy say?" she asked.

"He said that now that we only have a daddy that we might be dolphins," Henry explained. He looked down at his feet. "I don't mind though, 'cause that means we can swim real good."

47

"First of all, it's orphans, not dolphins, genius. And we aren't orphans anyway because we still have Daddy. Next time Malik says something like that, tell him to shut up." She was really beginning to hate that little brat.

"Ooooh!! 'Shut up' is a bad word, my teacher says!" Henry gave Serena a chastening look.

"Yeah, well, tell Malik to shut up anyway," Serena snapped. "We aren't orphans, okay?" Henry nodded unconvincingly. "And 'shut up' is two words."

Serena and Henry walked the last block to their house in silence—Serena reading her script when she was close enough to a streetlight, then trying to remember the words until the next lamp. Henry charged in front of her, holding a branch like a sword, leading his invisible troops into battle.

When they arrived at their house, they walked inside and dumped their stuff in the middle of the foyer.

"We're home!" Serena called.

There was no answer.

"Hello?"

"I'm going to give Daddy a kiss!" Henry announced. He took off up the stairs. Serena wanted to run up the stairs and give their father a kiss, too. But she didn't think she could stand it if he was still curled up on the bed crying like he was when they'd left that morning.

Henry reappeared quickly at the foot of the stairs.

"He's not in his room," he said, looking around as if their father would magically appear before them.

Great! Serena thought. *He finally got out of bed.* Grabbing her brother's hand, she headed down the stairs to the basement.

As she pushed open the door to her father's basement studio, Serena fully expected to see her father hunched over his desk, drawing away. When he was working, he could shut out just about everything. But her father wasn't at the desk drawing. He was sitting on the old, ratty couch in the corner of the room. He had his head in his hands and was wearing the same pajamas that he had been wearing this morning . . . and yesterday. And the day before that, come to think of it. Serena could tell he hadn't bothered to shave or shower because the room had a sort of musty, unwashed smell to it. Black and gray bristles stuck out from his usually clean-shaven chin.

"Daddy!" Henry shouted happily. He launched himself at their father, who caught him out of sheer reflex. Henry gave him a kiss on the cheek, seemingly oblivious to his smell. "Daddy, school today was so fun. Mrs. Duwee's daughter brought in her hermit crabs and we got to touch them. Then in gym we got to play tag, and I was so fast that no one could catch me. And then . . ." Henry talked and talked and talked.

Serena stood at the door watching her father closely.

He didn't seem to be paying any attention to Henry's torrent of words, patting him on the back absentmindedly.

". . . And that's why I'm starving. Oh, and Mrs. Duwee gave me this to give to you. Can I have a snack?" Their father nodded wearily and Henry plopped an envelope down on the desk, gave his father another kiss, and skipped out of the room.

Serena stood in the doorway and watched her father. If it weren't for the occasional blink he could have been dead.

"Daddy?" Serena asked, taking a step into the office. "Are you feeling better? Did you get some work done?"

"Yeah," he answered softly. Serena wasn't sure which question he was answering until he waved his hand toward a stack of packages sitting on the floor beside his desk.

"Oh, is that the art for the elephant book? You said I could see it before you sent it off."

"Oh, sorry," her father replied. "You can see the proofs when they come in."

Serena waited for him to say something, anything, about her phone call from school and her lead in the play. But he said nothing.

"So, now that I'm in the play," Serena said at last, "I can't pick Henry up from school, because I have rehearsal for two hours every single day. So you'll have to pick him up."

Her father nodded, but Serena really couldn't tell if he was listening. He sat staring straight ahead.

"Are you hungry, Daddy?" Serena asked. "Henry and I are going to make macaroni and cheese for dinner. Again," she added, feeling a little annoyed at the thought of having to eat boxed, neon orange pasta for the third night in a row.

Her father shook his head.

"Um, we need to go to the grocery store soon," Serena said. "We're kinda running out of food, and stuff." Her father only sighed.

Serena stood in the doorway for a few minutes. Then, with a sigh herself, she took a step out of the office and was about to walk up the stairs when her mother's last words to her floated into her head.

Take care of my boys, baby girl. Take care of them till I get home.

"Fine," Serena muttered. She took a step back into her father's office. "When was the last time you ate, Daddy?" she asked.

Her father looked up, startled. "Huh?"

"Food," Serena said, not bothering to tone down the sarcastic note in her voice. "When was the last time you had food in your mouth?"

Normally, her father would have told her not to be fresh. But then, things weren't normal anymore. They hadn't been since August 4, at 9:37 a.m.

"I don't know, baby," was all her father said, his voice muffled because he had returned his head to his hands.

"I'll bring you down some macaroni and cheese, okay?"

"Yeah, sure." Her father still didn't look in her direction. "I'm sorry, baby girl, I'm just feeling so out of it." He lay down on the couch and pulled himself into a ball. Serena waited for a moment to see if the crying would start. Thankfully, it didn't.

She left the office feeling worried. She hoped that his blue wasn't around to stay this time.

6

The next morning, Serena woke up with a page of Spanish homework pasted to her cheek. She had fallen asleep at her desk, and based on the big puddle in the middle of her verb translations, she'd drooled, too.

She'd also dreamed.

Since the past summer, Serena had begun to hate dreaming. Her dreams—her nightmares, to be more accurate— were never good. They weren't the type of nightmares she used to have, the kind with vampires and zombies and headless walking dolls. That all seemed like kid stuff now. Lately, she'd been reliving her mother's funeral. Or watching her father cry for days on end. Which was worse than vampires and zombies, because it was real. All completely and totally real. And in the morning, she always felt like she hadn't gotten any sleep at all.

Take care of my boys, baby girl. Take care of them till I get home.

Serena's dream last night had taken place in the funeral

home. She could see the coffin, and she could hear her mother's voice coming from inside of it.

Take care of my boys, baby girl. Take care of them till I get home.

Serena had tried to open the coffin lid to get her mother out. In her dream, she knew that if she could only open the lid, then her mother would climb out and everything would be okay. She would be alive and healthy and come back home. All Serena needed to do was to lift the lid of the coffin and let her out. But no matter how she tried, she couldn't lift the lid. It wouldn't budge, not at all.

Take care of my boys, baby girl. Take care of them till I get home.

Each time her mother said it, her voice got softer and softer. Serena knew that as soon as she stopped hearing her mother's voice, it would be too late to save her. She would be dead. Again.

Take care of my boys, baby girl. Take care of them till I get home.

Serena had called out to her father and Henry to help her lift the lid, but they'd simply stood there, looking helpless. That's when she'd noticed that they didn't have arms—they had legs, bodies, and heads, but no arms to help her lift the coffin lid. Serena had to do it herself, and she couldn't. The lid was too heavy.

Take care of my boys, baby girl. Take care of them till I get home.

Serena was running out of time. She looked wildly around for someone to help her. The only other person around was Malik, but he was a dolphin and his hands were fins. He laughed like a dolphin and flipped his fins together, which gave her the creeps.

Take care of my boys, baby girl. Take care of them till I get home.

Take care of my boys, baby girl. Take care of them till I get home.

Take care of my boys, baby girl. Take care of them till I get home.

Too late. Her mother died, again. Serena had failed. That's when she woke with a sob.

Yep, she definitely hated dreaming.

Shaking her head, Serena tried to get her dreams out of her mind. She looked at the clock and was relieved that she hadn't overslept. It was 5:29 a.m. Plenty of time to finish her homework, fix breakfast for Henry, get dressed, make sure her brother was ready, and head off to school. Her bed looked awfully comfortable, though, and her alarm wouldn't be ringing for another sixty-one, ooh, make that sixty, minutes. Serena knew she could get a lot done in that hour, but she also knew that she was butt tired. Looking longingly at her bed, she decided that if she couldn't actually sleep, she could at least finish her homework tucked cozily under her covers. She grabbed her schoolwork and made a nice nest with her pillow as a desk.

BEEP! BEEP! BEEP!

"*Crap!*" Serena said, slapping her alarm. "*Crap! Crap! Crap!*"

At that moment, Henry came bounding in the room.

"Crap's a 'don't say' word," he announced as he climbed onto the bed. He put a knee right in the center of her Spanish homework and gave her a hug.

"Hey! Off the bed, off! Get off!" Serena shouted, pushing him off her homework. Then she noticed what Henry was wearing.

"Henry, the shirt you have on is your pajama shirt, and it's cold out, so you need to find some long pants. And take off your soccer stuff and put on your regular tennis shoes. And 'crap' may be a bad word, but if I don't say it I will totally lose my mind. Go change, you look like a geek."

Henry stuck his lip out to show his disapproval, but walked out of the room without saying anything.

Serena called him back in. "Henry!"

He turned and looked at her.

She walked over to him and gave him a hug. "Good morning. Thank you for getting yourself up and getting dressed. It was very helpful."

Henry rewarded her with a big smile, then skipped out the door and down to his room.

"Find something a little warmer!" she called after him. "It's January."

Serena pulled the crumpled homework off her bed and reviewed which assignments she had done and which ones she still needed to complete. English reading, finished. Math, all done except for the last problem. Spanish, verb exercises done up until the drool spot in the middle of the page. Science reading, done. Social studies reading, not done. Serena stuffed everything into her backpack and double-checked to make sure that her script was safely inside as well.

After brushing her teeth and washing her face, Serena discovered all of her jeans were dirty. Her only other options were skirts. She chose a denim skirt that was just a little too tight. She grabbed a red sweater and was trying to decide what to do about shoes when Henry came wandering back in. His SpongeBob pajama shirt had been replaced with a soccer jersey, and his shorts had been replaced with too-short jeans.

"Dude, you've got on high-waters," Serena said.

"Huh?" Henry answered.

"Your pants are too short. Go find some others," Serena said, turning back to her closet to find some shoes that went with her outfit.

"I've only got fancy pants left," Henry told her.

Serena turned around and looked at him. "Really?"

"Yep," Henry said. "I'm hungry. Can I get some cereal?"

"Yeah, go ahead." *Gotta get the laundry done*, she told herself. Then she padded down the hall and knocked softly on her father's door.

"Please be up, please be up, please be up," she chanted softly to herself. When there was no answer, Serena opened the door and poked her head inside. The bedroom was empty.

"Yes!" she cheered.

Serena went directly to her mother's closet and flipped on the light. Everything was exactly the way it had been when her mother had left for her business trip—four days before that stupid truck ran into her while she was driving herself to the airport for her flight home. Her father hadn't touched a thing.

It took Serena a minute to find the shoebox she wanted. Then she turned off the closet light and hurried back to her room where she sat on her bed, the box on her lap. For a moment her eyes burned. She couldn't shake the feeling that she was doing something wrong. Taking a deep breath, she ripped off the top and pulled out a pair of red leather boots. They looked brand-new. Her mother had only worn them once or twice. Serena pulled them on. They fit perfectly.

You've got little feet and dainty hands, just like me, her mother had always told her. Serena closed her eyes. For a moment she could almost feel her mother's warm hand palm-to-palm with her own. She heard her mother's voice so clearly in her head that it made her heart ache.

Lord, I guess that means I'll have to share my shoes with you pretty soon, her mother had said, planting a kiss on her forehead.

Serena smiled at the memory. She placed her fingertips on the spot where her mother had regularly kissed her.

When she was fully dressed, Serena headed for the kitchen. Henry sat at the table in front of a bowl of Cap'n Crunch, munching loudly. Serena grabbed the last clean bowl, reminding herself to start the dishwasher before they left for school. She tilted the box and was rewarded with a spoonful of cereal dust.

"Hey!" she said, looking over at Henry accusingly.

"Sorry," said Henry through a mouthful of cereal

"No problem, just throw the empty box away. Don't put it back in the cupboard," Serena said, trying to shove the box into the overflowing trash can. *Empty the trash,* she thought, adding it to her list of things to do.

Heading back to the cupboard, she found that the only cereal left was her father's healthy cereal. Sighing, she poured some into her bowl. Then she yanked open the refrigerator door to get some milk.

"Whoa," she said, scanning the bare shelves. "We have got to get to the store."

She shut the refrigerator and looked at the kitchen table. "Henry, where's the milk?"

"There isn't any," he said, shoving another spoonful of cereal into his mouth.

"You used the last of that, too?" Serena was starting to get irritated.

Henry swallowed. "No," he said. "Wasn't any."

Serena peered into Henry's bowl. Sure enough, his cereal was bone-dry.

"We have *got* to get to the store," Serena said again. She dumped her cereal into the sink and opened the dishwasher, only to find that it was too full to add another dish. She added dishwasher soap and turned it on, then pulled out her script to study while Henry finished his breakfast.

While Henry was upstairs rewashing his face, Serena went back to the basement to talk to her father.

He was curled up on the couch asleep. For a split second, Serena hated him—hated that he could sleep so peacefully when she had so many bad dreams, hated that the plate of macaroni and cheese she'd brought down to him the night before was sitting hard and dry and untouched on his desk, hated that the laundry was undone and the refrigerator was almost empty while he did nothing all day. Standing there, watching him sleep, Serena wanted to scream. She closed her eyes and took a deep breath. She shook her clenched hands, wiggling her fingers to relax them. She wanted to walk over to her father and shake him. Shake him and shake him.

But why even bother? Serena walked over to her father's desk, pulled out his fancy drawing paper—the expensive kind that she wasn't allowed to use—and wrote him a note with one of his fancy coloring pencils.

Dear Dad,

   We are out of milk. We are out of clean clothes.
We are out of cereal. We are almost out of food.
Remember that I can't pick up Henry today. I have
rehearsal until 5:00.

                                                    Serena

She stuck the note on the floor right by the couch and
left. Her father didn't stir.

7

Getting through her classes, especially with rehearsal to look forward to at the end of the day, was hard. Not that there weren't highlights. Serena's name and starring role were mentioned during the morning announcements, and people in her first-period class actually applauded for her. And when she walked into Spanish, Elijah whistled and said, "You look hot in that skirt, *chica!* *Y pensé que tu no podrías ser más bonita.*"

Naturally, she had poked him with her pencil as a punishment for speaking Spanish, although she secretly liked the whistling. She modeled her outfit for him briefly, before pleading with him to let her "borrow" his Spanish homework again.

"Dang, girl," Elijah said with a laugh. "You keep this up, you are going to owe me a serious favor."

"As often as you've saved my butt lately, you are welcome to it," Serena answered while she hurriedly copied the last of the homework.

"Really?" Elijah said. "I'm welcome to your butt?"

"Boy, shut up!" Serena said, sliding his homework back to him.

"Hay algo que usted quiere compartir con la clase, Señorita Shaw?" said Miss Capra.

"Um, no?" Serena answered. Serena never felt quite sure she understood what Miss Capra was saying. She liked to hedge her bets and give noncommittal answers whenever possible.

"Entonces por favor esté quieta para que puedo empezar la clase," Miss Capra said sternly. She looked at Serena, clearly waiting for an answer. But all Serena had understood was *"por favor"* and *"clase."*

"Um, *sí?*" she answered hesitantly.

Miss Capra gave her a quick nod before turning back to the board. Serena heaved a sigh and slunk down in her seat. Elijah's shoulders shook with silent laughter. Serena leaned forward and flicked him in the back of the neck.

After Spanish, Elijah walked with Serena to the lunchroom. They stood side by side, pushing their trays along, talking about the play.

"Your debt to me keeps adding up, Serena Star," Elijah said as he plopped an apple on his tray.

"How do you figure?" Serena asked, reaching over him to grab a ham sandwich.

"Well, there's the constant need for my Spanish expertise, and now, suddenly, I'm the artistic director of your

63

play." Elijah let Serena slide past him to the register since he was still busy loading his tray with food.

"Whoa, hold up there, Picasso," Serena said. "Seems to me you would forget about the debt, since we are close personal friends and all."

"Oh, see, now you're tripping," Elijah said. They both paid for their food and left the lunch line.

Serena looked around the lunchroom. "Yeah, well, my favor is listening to you talk Spanish all the dang time," she told him.

"Don't think you'll get off that easy," Elijah answered with a grin. "Later, Serena Star." And he left to sit with his boys.

Serena considered her seating options. To her left sat Candy and a couple of other people from the play. To her right were Kat and Nikka. She really wanted to head to the left. She wasn't in the mood to hear her best friends' mouths. Of course, *not* sitting with them would make things even worse. So, with a sigh, Serena headed to the right, plopping down in the seat next to Kat.

"Girl, where have you been?" Nikka asked, pointing an accusing French fry at Serena. "Feels like I ain't seen you in, like, forever."

"Um, hello! I've been here at school." Serena snatched the fry out of Nikka's hand and shoved it in her own mouth. "Not that I could say the same about you. Besides, I saw you, like, yesterday. Stop acting like it's been a grip of time."

"Uh, you're welcome, greedy gut," Nikka said. She picked up another fry. "It's like you're never around anymore. Too big a star to hang with us no more?"

"Girl, don't even start," Serena snapped. "We've had a total of one rehearsal."

Nikka always wanted to start drama.

"Look, I gotta keep it on the low-key tip until the play is over. And my grades can't slip or they'll kick me out."

"Whatever, Miss Diva," Nikka answered. "I don't know why you want to be in that whacked-out play no way." She looked over at Kat, who simply shrugged.

"Do you not listen?" Serena replied. The last thing she needed right now was Nikka and her negative attitude. "What have I been talking about since we started middle school?"

"Being in the musicals," Kat answered. Nikka rolled her eyes.

"And what have I been talking about since the school year started?"

"Trying out for the musical," Kat said.

"And what have I been talking about ever since they announced that this year's play was *The Wiz*?"

"Being the star of the musical," Kat chirped. She turned to Nikka. "I don't know why you trippin' like this, Nikka. You the one who told her if you had to hear about that doggone play one more time you were going to go off on her. Now you acting like this whole thing is a big surprise. Besides, our girl is the star. The leading lady. That is too tight."

"Yeah, well, whatever," Nikka said lamely. "Maybe when this stupid thing is over, you can go back to listening to regular music again, instead of that whacked-out Broadway mess you always humming."

"Whatever," Kat answered back. "Don't be hatin', that's all I'm saying. Serena, I'll be front row center."

"Thanks, Kat," Serena said. "You my girl."

The rest of lunch passed peacefully enough, but to Serena the vibe felt uneasy and awkward. Nikka's only contributions to the conversation were negative and cutting—as usual. Serena was glad when the bell rang for fifth period.

In English, Serena fought the urge to slump down and half listen the way she normally did, but she thought that maybe, just maybe, with a little more effort she could drag her grade to a B–. If she participated a little more in English maybe her improved grade would balance her deteriorating Spanish one, to keep her grade point average steady.

"Okay, class, let's talk about chapter seven of *The Outsiders*," Mrs. Knight said. "Who would like to give me a synopsis?"

Serena held up her hand.

Mrs. Knight called on her with raised eyebrows.

"Um, after the two boys save those kids from the burning building all their friends visit them at the hospital," Serena started. "And then the greasers say that Johnny killed Bob only because he was protecting himself." She paused, thinking about her reading the night before. "So then they find out that Soda's girlfriend is going to have a baby and then they decide not to fight anymore."

"Correct. Excellent job, Serena," Mrs. Knight said.

Serena smiled as Mrs. Knight made a mark in her grade book. Her class participation done, Serena slid down in her seat and tried to look like she was paying attention.

AFTER WHAT SEEMED LIKE AN ETERNITY, THE FINAL BELL rang. Serena hurried to her locker, grabbed her things, and headed to the auditorium.

She was anxious to get started. Even before Mr. Hobbs appeared, Serena made everyone begin rehearsing. In no time, she, Candy, and Donnie, who played Uncle Henry, were running lines. Serena knew she was being a little bossy, but she didn't care. The play felt like it was *hers*, and she wanted to do everything she could to make it good. Besides, play rehearsal was the one place in her life where she felt like she had total control.

Serena and Candy knew almost all of their lines for the scene, but Donnie read everything in a flat monotone. When Elijah appeared, Serena only gave him a quick wave before going right back to rehearsing. She was determined to have Donnie off book by the end of rehearsal. But after only fifteen minutes or so, Mr. Hobbs called her over to the piano to work on one of her songs.

"Okay, Miss Shaw, let's try 'Home.' It's the biggest number, so I want to make sure you have it down cold. If it's done right it can be a showstopper. First let's go over the words."

"Oh, I know all the words," Serena told him.

Mr. Hobbs tilted his head. "You think so, eh?"

"I do, scout's honor," Serena said. She cleared her throat and began to sing. Mr. Hobbs quickly found her key and began accompanying her.

"When I think of home I think of a place, where there's love overflowing," she sang. Closing her eyes, she imagined her mom sitting on the couch, her dad's arms wrapped around her. Henry was sprawled at the other end of the couch. They were all laughing.

"I wish I was home. I wish I was back there, with the things I've been knowing."

And as she sang, instead of suppressing all the emotions that had been building up since her dad's blue began to reappear, Serena sang it all out—transferring to Dorothy all her worry, all of her anger, and all of her sadness. And as she sang, Serena's frustrations and fears melted away.

"Like home . . ."

She sang the last words of the song and opened her eyes. She felt lighter, as if all her burdens had somehow been lifted. When the last piano note faded into the air, Serena became aware of the deep silence in the auditorium.

She looked around. Every single person had stopped what they were doing. And they were all staring at her. Elijah sat motionless, holding a paintbrush in his hand and dripping yellow paint all over the brick road he'd been creating. He had a goofy grin on his face. If he laughed at her, she was going to find a plastic fork and . . .

But before she could finish her thought, someone started clapping. Then everyone joined in, and the auditorium echoed with applause.

"Serena, that was incredible," Mr. Hobbs said. "You sang your heart out. You infused each word, each musical phrase, with emotion. I can see that grant check now!"

Serena grinned. She couldn't remember the last time she had felt so happy.

"All right, then," Mr. Hobbs went on. "Let's try 'Soon as I Get Home.' Now this song—"

Before he could finish his sentence, a bang echoed from the back of the auditorium. The doors had slammed shut and Mrs. Vickers, the school secretary, was hurrying down the aisle.

She walked quickly, heading straight toward Mr. Hobbs and Serena.

"I'm so sorry to interrupt," Mrs. Vickers said, "but I just got a call from Harrington Elementary about Serena's little brother."

Serena looked down at her watch. It was 3:45. Henry should have been home by now. With Daddy.

"Is he okay? Did he get hurt or something?" Serena asked. Her stomach began to twist into knots.

"Oh, no, he's not hurt, but someone needs to pick him up," Mrs. Vickers said. "The teacher called your house and no one answered. Your brother said that your dad was sick and he thought perhaps you would be picking him up."

"Oh, well, my dad isn't feeling, um, like himself," Serena said. "But I left him a note this morning about Henry. Are they sure he didn't answer the phone?" Mrs. Vickers nodded. "I told him that I had rehearsal," Serena said softly. "I did."

"Hey, now, it's okay," Mr. Hobbs said. "How about I drive you over there real quick and pick him up? He can hang out here until rehearsal is over. Assuming he won't be disruptive."

Serena breathed a sigh of relief. "Oh, would you please, Mr. Hobbs? He'll be real behaved." At least she hoped he would be, or she'd have to kill him.

"Of course, grab your coat."

The drive from Grove to Harrington was quick. Serena ran up the school steps two at a time, and hurried down the empty hallways toward Henry's room. Pushing the door open, she could see Mrs. Duwee, her coat on, arms crossed. Henry was watching the classroom gerbil play on his wheel.

"I'm so sorry, Mrs. Duwee!" Serena said, hurrying into the room. "My dad and I had a bit of a mix-up."

"Things like this happen," the teacher said. "I wouldn't have called you, but I couldn't get in touch with your father."

"I'm really, really sorry," Serena said. "My dad, he hasn't been feeling well, but I thought he'd pick up Henry. I'm so sorry."

Mrs. Duwee's face softened some. "Well, please make sure that you have everything organized for the rest of the week," she said. "I sometimes stay a while after school, but this month is a bit busy for me. So if you could make sure that someone arrives promptly, I would greatly appreciate it."

Serena nodded, a hopeless feeling washing over her. Clearly she couldn't depend on her father to pick Henry up. How could she do it every day *and* get to rehearsal?

As Mrs. Duwee headed for the door she turned and said, "Oh, and by the way. I sent a letter home with Henry yesterday. Do you know whether your father got it or not?"

"Um," Serena mumbled. She thought back to the letter she'd seen that morning sitting under the plate of dried-up macaroni and cheese on her father's desk. "I know that Henry gave it to him," she said weakly.

"Please tell your father that the letter is very important," said Mrs. Duwee. "As soon as he's feeling better, he should call me to discuss it. Can you handle that message?"

"Yes, ma'am," Serena said, pulling Henry toward the door. "I will."

As they walked out of the school toward Mr. Hobbs's waiting car, Henry said, "I'm sorry, Serena. Are you mad at me? You look mad."

"No," Serena said, taking his hand and giving it a little squeeze. "No, I'm not mad at *you*. Not mad at you at all."

8

After rehearsal, Serena and Henry found their father sitting at the dining room table, staring at the family picture that hung over the side table. It had been taken a month before her mother's accident. One of the last things her mother had done before leaving on her business trip was tell Serena's father exactly where she wanted it. Serena had watched the whole scene unfold from the doorway.

"No, baby, not on that wall, this one over here," she had said.

"Are you sure? I thought we discussed hanging it over there." Her father had huffed as he lugged the heavy frame over to the other side of the dining room.

"Well, we did, but I was thinking that it would look better over here."

"Yeah, but then we have to move all those other pictures," Serena's father answered. "Besides, I'm the artist of the family. I think I should have the final say of where it looks best."

Her mother had raised an eyebrow and sat down in a dining room chair to wait. Serena's father walked around the room, carefully looking at all the available wall space and back at the picture. Finally, he'd said, "You know, I think it will look best right here." Then, clearing his throat, he pointed to the exact space Serena's mother had picked out ten minutes before.

Her mother burst out laughing. "Gee, I wish I had your artistic eye," she said, kissing her husband on the cheek. "You can fix it while I'm gone, and surprise me with it when I get back."

"Oh, I can, can I?" Serena's father said with a laugh. He set the picture down and pulled her to him.

"Yes, you can," her mother answered, standing on her tiptoes to give him another kiss. "I'd be very, very grateful."

At that point Serena had walked away. Who wants to see their parents all kissy-faced?

Her mother never saw the picture in its new place.

Serena dropped her backpack on the floor so loudly it caused her father to jump. A rush of irritation flooded her. Where was his mind that he couldn't hear Henry's big ole mouth yammering away as they walked through the door?

It used to be that when Serena and Henry got home from school, their father would greet them at the door with bear hugs and demand to know what they had done all day. He'd fix them an afternoon snack and listen to Henry talk and talk and talk. Then, while they ate, he'd shush Henry and ask Serena about her classes. "What did you learn today? What made you mad? What made you laugh?"

All that seemed like a long time ago now.

Henry, however, didn't seem fazed by their father's inattentiveness. He crawled up into his father's lap and launched into a story about how he got to spend extra time with the class gerbil, Nibbles, because no one came to pick him up after school.

That comment seemed to break through her father's fog and he looked away from the family portrait over to Serena.

"I was supposed to pick him up, wasn't I?" her father asked her quietly. He buried his head in Henry's neck. "Oh, baby boy, I'm so sorry."

Finally! Serena thought. Her father's haze had been lifted.

"That's okay, Daddy," Henry said. "I got to fill Nibbles's water bottle and I went to Serena's hearsal and painted the yellow brick road to Oz. *And*, Elijah said I can come every day and help him paint if I want to."

"It's *re*hearsal," Serena said, "not hearsal, and Elijah told you what?" Serena was ignoring the pained, sad look on her father's face. She didn't want to feel sorry for him. She wanted to be angry.

75

"He said we could work on the road together every day if I wanted. He also said to tell you that me and him were, um, emgos? And that the flavors were piling up."

"Emgos?" Serena said. "What the heck are—ohhh, *amigos*." She smiled despite herself. "And it's *favors*, not flavors, goofball."

"Yeah, *amigos*. That's what I just said. Can I get something to eat?" Henry bounced out of the room.

"Dad," Serena said, turning to her father, "did you go to the grocery store?"

Her father ran a hand across his face before slowly shaking his head.

"Great, what are we going to have for dinner then? What are we supposed to eat for breakfast tomorrow? We are seriously out of food."

Her father sighed. "Just order some pizza, 'kay? I'll go tonight. Or tomorrow morning. I'm so . . ." Pulling his face out of his hands, he turned to Serena, and for the first time his eyes fell on the shoes she was wearing—her mother's red leather boots.

"Take. Those. Off."

Her father's voice sounded strangled, almost guttural. Serena took a step back.

"I said, take those off now, young lady."

Serena sat down in the nearest dining room chair and pulled off the boots as quickly as she could. Her father reached out and snatched them away from her.

"These are Vi's," her father said softly, hugging them to his chest.

Serena turned and walked out of the room without responding.

MUCH LATER THAT NIGHT, AFTER HENRY HAD BEEN FED, bathed, and put to bed, and Serena had finished all her homework, even Spanish (Ha! Take that Elijah!), she went downstairs to her father's office. There, on the desk, still covered by the plate of old macaroni and cheese, was the envelope. Serena picked up the plate and the envelope and headed to the kitchen. She opened the dishwasher to stick the plates in, only to find it still full of the now-clean dishes from this morning.

Slamming the plate down, she tossed the letter on the counter and set about emptying the dishwasher. Then she swept the floor and wiped down the counters. Twenty minutes later, she collapsed into a chair and surveyed her work. She felt a brief surge of pride at the spotless kitchen. When her mother was alive, Serena had pretended to hate helping her in the kitchen. But really, it had been kinda fun. They would sing together while they worked, picking show tunes from one of the musicals they'd watched on TV.

Serena was happily caught up in her memories for a moment, until she remembered that neither she nor Henry had any clean clothes to wear tomorrow. She'd have to do laundry before she went to bed.

She heaved a sigh and jogged up the stairs, tiptoeing quietly into Henry's room. His night-light cast enough of a glow that she could easily reach his overflowing laundry basket without stepping on any Legos or action figures. *If Mom could see this mess she would just flip!* she thought for a second, until she remembered what Henry had told her the day before. A big lump appeared in her throat and her eyes filled with tears. Blinking furiously, she picked up the basket and headed to the door, stopping briefly to watch Henry sleep. A trickle of drool was seeping out of the corner of his mouth. Serena felt a stab of jealousy, wishing her nights could be as restful as Henry's. Sighing, she closed his door softly and headed to her room to get her own dirty clothes.

As she passed her father's bedroom she paused. He would probably have a basket full of dirty clothes as well. Then it occurred to her that actually, he probably wouldn't, since all he seemed to want to wear was the same pair of dingy pajamas. She walked on past. Her father was way older than twelve. He would have to wash his own clothes.

Serena lugged the clothes down the two flights of stairs into the basement laundry room. A glance at the clock told her it was already 9:47. She knew she would have to do at least two loads of laundry—one set of whites and one for jeans and shirts. She separated the clothes and then crammed the whites into the machine until it was nearly full.

The day after Serena's twelfth birthday, her mother had called her into the laundry room and announced that she was now in charge of doing her own laundry. Then she'd given her a ten-minute tutorial about sorting and temperature selection, along with a laundry cheat sheet, which was still taped on the wall behind the washing machine.

Hot = white
Cold = dark
Warm = anything in between

At the time, Serena had been honestly irritated. She couldn't believe her mother was so mean —after all, all her friends' moms still washed their clothes. But now all those laundry lessons were coming in awfully handy.

She sat down next to the washer with her script to study her lines guilt-free, having finally finished her homework for once.

SERENA WAS IN THE MIDDLE OF A STRANGE WOOD, *following a road of yellow dirt. In the distance ahead she could see a figure walking slowly away from her. It was her mother. Serena opened her mouth to call to her, but no matter how hard she tried, no sound came out, and no matter how quickly she walked, her mother only got farther and farther away. Again she opened her mouth to scream to her mother to stop, to wait for her. Nothing. Her mother was fading away. Serena opened her mouth one more time and out came—*

BEEP! BEEP! BEEP!

Serena awoke with a start, not realizing at first where she was.

BEEP! BEEP! BEEP!

She was leaning against the laundry room wall, surrounded by dirty clothes. Then she remembered. She pulled the clean white load out of the dryer and dumped everything into a basket. Then she put the wet dark load into the dryer and turned it on.

Serena thought briefly about brushing her teeth before climbing into bed, but she was too tired. Burrowing down into her covers, she reached over and set her alarm for fifteen minutes earlier than usual.

THE NEXT MORNING, SERENA WOKE UP EXHAUSTED. AFTER dumping Henry's clean but seriously wrinkled clothes onto the foot of his bed and starting a load of towels, she had a realization. She had to get some help. And it wasn't going to come from Henry or her father.

Serena walked into her father's office, clicked on the lights, and quickly found her father's address book in one of his desk drawers. It was time to call the two relatives she had left—her grandmother and her uncle Peter, both on

80

her father's side. Her grandma used to visit all the time, until a few years ago when she had begun to get really forgetful and flighty. Her uncle was some bigwig, hotshot business guy who traveled all over the world. They only saw him every once in a while but he always sent them really cool gifts. Serena figured that telling problems to her own family was okay. It wasn't airing their personal affairs if it was family.

Serena flipped through the address book until she found her uncle's name: Peter C. Shaw, Esq. She dialed, but the call went to voice mail.

"Hello, you've reached Peter Shaw, Senior Vice President of Foreign Mineral Acquisitions. Unfortunately I'm not available at the moment. If this is concerning the Brazilian ore acquisitions, please call Gustavo de Santana at the home office. Otherwise please leave a message at the tone. Thank you."

What should Serena's message be? "Hey, Uncle Peter, wherever in the world you are, please come home and fix your brother"? She sighed and waited for the beep.

"Hi, Uncle Peter, it's Serena. Um, I just wanted to let you know that I got the leading role in the play at school. I'm Dorothy in *The Wiz*. It's the second weekend in March, and you have to be there. No matter what. Have your secretary put that date on your schedule. Okay, I guess that's all. Love you. Bye."

Next she dialed the number listed under Sophia Shaw.

"Hello, Seminole Assisted Care Home, offering the best in assisted and memory care. This is Marjorie, how may I help you?" a crisp voice said.

Serena was stunned for a moment. When had her grandmother moved? Thinking back, she could dimly remember a few discussions between her parents, and some trips down south that her father had made. But then her mother had died and she'd stopped paying much attention to anything else. The last time she had seen her grandmother was at the funeral.

"Hello?" said the voice. "Hello?"

"Oh, yes, sorry." Serena shook it off. "Um, may I please speak with Sophia Shaw?"

"Certainly, one moment please while I connect you."

After a moment Serena heard her grandmother's voice. "Hello?"

"Hi!" Serena clutched the phone tightly. "Hi, it's me."

"Vivian, sweetie, how are you?" her grandmother said. "It's so nice to hear from you!"

"No, no," Serena said. "It's me! Sere—"

"Yes, I know it's you, Vivian. I could tell right away. How's my boy treating you? You tell him he better be a good husband or I'll come right up there and give him a whopping." Her grandmother laughed.

"Now how are those babies doing? Ohh! I bet they're growing like weeds."

"Grandma?" Serena said softly. But her grandmother didn't seem to hear her.

"Grandma?" Serena shouted into the receiver. "It's me. It's Serena, Grandma."

"Serena? That you, sweetie? How you doing, baby? Oh, I bet you're getting up on legs, like we used to say. You being a help to your mother?"

"Mom's dead, Grandma," Serena said flatly. "Remember?"

"Dead?" her grandma wailed. "*Oh, my God, no! Oh, Lord Jesus, no!*"

"Grandma! Grandma!" Serena shouted. "She died last year! Don't you remember? You came to her funeral? In August! Grandma?"

But her grandmother didn't answer. Serena heard the phone drop.

"Grandma! Grandma!" Serena shouted. She could hear her grandmother wailing.

She heard the phone being picked up.

"Who is this?" asked an angry voice.

"Um, it's Serena?" she answered. "I'm Sophia's granddaughter. Is she okay?"

"Well, she's extremely upset. Can you tell me what happened?"

"Nothing," Serena explained. "I mean, she thought I was my mother, but my mother died more than a year ago. My grandma knows that. She came to the funeral. I was

83

just trying to tell her that we need her to visit. My dad, my brother, and I, we need her. She needs to come stay with us for a while. We need help."

"Oh, honey," said the voice with pity. "Your grandmother's got Alzheimer's and sometimes she doesn't remember things too well. I'm afraid she isn't well enough to leave the facility right now, either. I'm so sorry. But she's calmed down now. Would you like to speak with her again?"

Serena swallowed before saying, "Yes, please."

"All right, dear. I'll put her on. And I'm sorry about your mother's passing. It's awful to lose a parent so young."

"Thank you, ma'am," Serena replied.

After a moment her grandmother came back on the line. "Hello?"

"Hi, Grandma," Serena said, crossing her fingers. "It's me, Serena."

"Serena, baby, is that you?" Serena could hear her talking to the nurse. "It's my grandbaby, Serena!"

"Hi, Grandma," Serena said again. "How are you?"

"Oh, baby, I'm doing just fine. I'm here at this hotel, though I must say, I've stayed in nicer ones. Nothing but old people in this one. How are things with you, sweetie?" her grandma said. "I bet you growing like a weed."

After talking to her grandmother for five minutes about pretty much nothing, Serena headed to the bathroom to wipe the tears from her face, because this time, when the tears came, she hadn't been able to stop them.

9

All morning long Serena was preoccupied, hardly paying any attention in class. She was trying to figure out what to do about picking Henry up. She'd been in such a hurry before she left for school, she hadn't gotten a chance to remind her father about it, and naturally he hadn't come out of his room to see them off.

Finally lunch rolled around, and for the second time that week Serena found herself rushing to the office to call her father. But after the fifth time the phone went to voice mail she gave up.

Walking like a zombie to the lunchroom, Serena felt the beginnings of a headache. How was she supposed to be in two places at the same time?

"Hey, girl! Over here!" Kat called over the din of the cafeteria. She was waving her arms in the air to catch Serena's attention.

Serena walked to the table and sat down. The smell of the French fries on Kat's plate made her stomach growl.

There hadn't been any time or food for breakfast that morning. Her stomach roared again, even louder.

"Dang, girl," Nikka said with a laugh. "I thought you was supposed to be Dorothy, not the Cowardly Lion." Kat laughed, too, but pushed her plate over toward Serena, who grabbed a couple of fries.

"What is up with you?" Nikka asked. "Why is your face all busted?"

"Henry," Serena answered.

"What's the matter with Henry?" Kat asked.

"Naw, he's all right. It's just that I have to pick him up from school," Serena answered quietly. Between her hunger and her tiredness she felt like she was talking to her friends through a haze. She shook her head, trying to clear her thoughts, but all she wanted to do was put her head down and take a nap.

"Yeah, so what?" Nikka picked up an untouched cup of applesauce from her tray and shoved it over to Serena, who had finished off Kat's fries.

"I gotta be at rehearsal right after school, that's what. It takes like fifteen minutes to walk to Harrington Elementary, and another five just to pick him up, and then another fifteen minutes to get back here," Serena told them. "That's a long time not to be at rehearsal, especially if you're the lead."

"Especially if you're the lead," Nikka mimicked.

"So unnecessary, Nikka," Kat said, shoving an unopened carton of milk over to Serena. "What about your dad? Doesn't he still work from home?"

"No thanks," Serena said, pushing the carton back in Kat's direction. "You know I hate milk. And he does work from home, but, um, he's not doing so good." For a moment she wanted to tell her friends about her dad. About how he barely got out of bed, the dingy pajamas, and the crying. She opened her mouth to tell them everything that was going on at home, but then caught a glimpse of Nikka looking unsympathetic and irritated. Knowing what a gossip Nikka was, Serena had no doubt all of her dirty laundry would be in every part of the school before the final bell rang. People had just stopped looking at her all funny because of her mom; she didn't want to deal with the pitying looks she was sure to get if people found out her dad had flipped. Better keep her problems to herself. Serena scooped a spoonful of applesauce into her mouth instead.

"Oh, he got the flu?" Kat asked. "My mom says there's a bad one going around." Her mother was a nurse and was always warning the girls about some new medical danger—the swine flu, ticks, salmonella, mad cow disease. "Did you guys get the flu shot? Maybe your dad has it."

"Yeah, he's got a bug or something," Serena lied. "But what can I do about Henry?"

Nikka shrugged. "Sounds like you're screwed. Just run over there and back."

Serena nodded glumly. What other choice did she have?

"We'll pick him up," Kat said brightly.

"Who's 'we'?" Nikka snapped, shooting an angry glare over at Kat. Kat rolled her eyes.

Serena ignored Nikka, too. "Oh, will you really?" she asked Kat. "That would be wonderful."

"Yeah, no prob," Kat said.

Nikka heaved a loud and dramatic sigh. "Hello? Miss Do-Gooder," she said. "We're supposed to meet those two hotties from the high school at the coffeehouse after school today, remember?"

Serena turned to Nikka with raised eyebrows. "Whoa, what two hotties? What's up? What'd I miss?" She looked at Kat. "What about Charles?"

"Girl, Charles is so yesterday," Kat said. "On to bigger, better, and *so* much cuter pastures."

"Dang, I'm sorry I missed all this stuff," Serena said.

"Oh, like you care," Nikka snapped. "You think 'cause you're too busy to hang, we can't do nothing fun until you have time for us? That day *you* were too good to ditch with us, Kat and I met a couple of honeys at the coffee-house. Marcus and the other one, whatever his name is . . ."

"Ian," Kat offered.

"Yeah, that's it," Nikka continued. "Marcus and Ian. We set up a little date. We might even head to the movies after our frappaccinos!"

Serena felt a stab of jealousy. She had never had a date in her life, much less with a high school guy. She looked over at Kat to make sure that Nikka wasn't exaggerating, but Kat was cheesing from ear to ear and nodding in agreement.

"The movies?" Serena said, trying to sound casual. "Wow. I don't want to make you guys miss your date or anything."

"Girl, please," Kat said. "Trust me, they *will* wait for us. We'll bring Henry back here and then stroll into the coffeehouse like we ain't geeked to be hooking up with them. It'll help us look chilled, you know?"

"That would be so great," Serena said. She turned toward Nikka with a sad puppy-dog look on her face. "I'd really owe you a big one. Please, Nikka!"

"Oh, Lord, don't even give me that sad-ass look." Nikka rolled her eyes again. "Oh, for crying out loud, fine, whatever," she added with a short laugh. "No wonder you got the lead in that funky play, Miss Drama Queen. We'll get your little brother. But if Marcus and what's-his-name leave before we come strolling in looking cute, I swear I'll come to every single one of your performances and boo at you like it's the Apollo Theatre on amateur night."

"You guys are the best! Thank you, thank you!" Serena said. She suddenly felt like she could breathe a little deeper. "I better call his teacher and let her know you guys are coming." And she set off, back to the phone in the school office.

WHEN THE LAST BELL FINALLY RANG, SERENA DRAGGED herself to the auditorium. As excited as she was about rehearsal, she was exhausted, and her stomach was growling again. She slumped down in a front-row seat and willed herself not to fall asleep. A short ten minutes later the rest of the cast had appeared and Serena ignored her fatigue and got busy rehearsing.

Every few minutes she would glance to the rear of the auditorium, worried that Nikka had persuaded Kat to blow off picking up Henry. Serena could tell that Candy was trying to catch her eye, to give her emotional support, but she didn't need her sympathy. What she needed were her best friends to come bursting into the auditorium with her little brother.

"Serena! Serena!"

Mr. Hobbs was calling her. Serena stopped running lines with Eriq, the Scarecrow, and headed down to the front of the auditorium.

"Let's do a few of your songs," Mr. Hobbs said, settling himself down on the piano. "I want to start really polishing the phrasing and arrangement." He played a flourish but Serena just nodded. She was so tired that even the idea of singing didn't appeal to her. All she wanted to do was take a nap.

As Mr. Hobbs played "Ease on Down the Road," Serena started singing, but he stopped her after only a few bars.

"Your voice sounds a little weak today, Serena. You aren't getting sick, are you? We really can't afford to have our star miss any rehearsal time. We are on an extremely tight schedule. You don't think you're catching what your father's got, do you?"

"No, no, Mr. Hobbs," Serena said. *Definitely not*, she thought to herself. She cleared her throat. "I just didn't sleep that well last night."

"Well, you *have* to get sleep," Mr. Hobbs told her. "I can't have my star run-down. That's how you get sick."

At that moment Serena heard Henry's voice coming from the back of the auditorium. He was walking down the aisle holding on to Kat's hand, swinging it wildly back and forth. Kat didn't seem to mind. Nikka stayed by the door, arms crossed. Kat stopped midway down the aisle, gave Henry a quick hug, then trotted back to Nikka. They left without a wave.

Henry sauntered down to where Serena was. "I'm hungry," he announced.

Mr. Hobbs looked down at Henry for a moment. Then he turned to Serena with a questioning expression on his face.

Serena hurried to explain. "Oh, Mr. Hobbs, I meant to ask if it was okay if Henry could hang out here again. It's, he, I—" Serena stammered. "See, it's just that with my

91

dad not feeling well, I haven't figured out anywhere for him, for Henry, to go after school, so I was hoping it'd be all right for him to hang out here. He won't be a problem."

"Serena," Mr. Hobbs said, running his hand across his hair. "I'm fighting to save this program. I don't have the time to focus on anything but making our production worthy of the grant. We've got quite a lot of work to get done in just a few weeks. And this isn't a day care. I mean yesterday, fine, but if this is going to be an everyday occurrence . . . Maybe a babysitter would be better for him."

"I'm not a baby," Henry announced. He was scowling at Mr. Hobbs.

"Boy, fix your face," Serena hissed. Had Henry lost his mind? This was completely unlike him.

Mr. Hobbs, however, did something Serena didn't expect. He stuck his tongue out at Henry.

Henry, not missing a beat, stuck his tongue out right back.

Mr. Hobbs crossed his eyes and stuck his fingers in his ears. Henry mimicked him, crossing his eyes as best he could, and sticking his fingers in his ears. Mr. Hobbs puffed out his cheeks and thumbed his nose at Henry. Henry did it right back. Serena watched in silence, fascinated.

At last Mr. Hobbs roared with laughter. "Your brother

may stay," he told Serena. "As long as he isn't disruptive, that's fine."

Serena pointed Henry toward a row of seats. "Sit down, don't move, don't say a single word, don't bother anyone, don't touch anything, and don't you dare make any noise," she told him.

Henry frowned at her. "I'm hungry," he muttered, slumping down in a seat. "I want a snack."

Serena nodded. She was hungry, too. But she didn't want to be any more trouble than she already was

"Hey, little man! Henry!" someone called from the stage. "Yo, dude, come up here! I have a chore for you, *mi amigo*."

It was Elijah, waving from the stage, where several sets-in-progress were scattered about. He jogged down to talk to them.

"Hey, Serena, Mr. Hobbs, can Henry help me? I'm a little shorthanded up there. I could use the extra hands." He winked at Henry and tossed him a candy bar.

"Oh, I don't know," Serena said hesitantly, ignoring the low growling of her stomach that had started again at the sight of Henry devouring his candy bar. She looked over at Mr. Hobbs.

"Well . . ." Mr. Hobbs began uncertainly.

"It'll be fine," Elijah told them, pulling a rolled-up notebook from his back pocket. "According to my production schedule, I'm only doing the base painting for the next couple of days. He can help with that no problem. After that's finished I'll start on the detail work—focus on making the different sets pop the way they should."

"According to your schedule?" Serena said, cocking an eyebrow at Elijah. She was impressed. Of course, she'd never tell him that.

"Yes," Elijah said. "My schedule. Henry did great yesterday, Mr. Hobbs, very meticulous, and I'm short stagehands. Half of my crew bailed after only one day."

"Meticulous?" Serena asked. "Did you just say 'meticulous'? Who are you?" Elijah simply winked at her.

"Please, Serena. Please!" Henry whined, bouncing on the toes of his feet.

Serena shrugged and looked over at Mr. Hobbs.

"Hey, I've been doing these school plays for fifteen years, and in fifteen years not once have I witnessed an artistic director who had a schedule—even the adult ones. As far as I'm concerned, young man, you may do whatever you want. Now, Miss Shaw," he continued, as Henry and Elijah slapped each other five as the little boy scurried up the stage steps, "let's get back to easing down the yellow brick road, shall we?"

Serena returned to her place by the piano, but when she heard Elijah call her name, she turned to look back at him.

"So, Serena Star," he said, smiling. "How many favors is that now?"

10

With her head hurting and her body heavy from tiredness, Serena found the walk home with Henry after rehearsal seemed twice as long as usual. All Serena wanted to do was eat, take a bath, and crawl into bed. Henry was unusually quiet, which allowed her mind to drift. Pictures of what Fridays had been like popped into her head.

Before, when her mother was still alive, Fridays had been Favorite Food Fridays. Henry's Friday food of choice had always been pizza. Serena's choice changed monthly, ranging from hamburgers to shrimp scampi to breakfast for dinner. Her father's Friday food depended on what sort of illustrations he was working on at the moment. When he'd been working on the picture book about the spaghetti-loving boy named Sam, they'd had spaghetti. When the book was about Temple, the peanut-loving elephant, they'd had peanut butter and jelly sandwiches. Mom's Friday had *always* meant a dinner at a nice restaurant. Four people, each with their own special Friday meal every month. It was Serena's mother's way of making ordinary weeks a little special. When she died, on that hot, sunny Tuesday morning in August, it had been before Serena's Friday dinner of burgers, fries, and root beer floats.

This Friday, Serena and Henry arrived at home to find a quiet, dark house. No lights on to welcome them, no hot food waiting for them on the dining room table. Serena flicked on the hallway light and leaned against the wall, too tired to take another step. Henry dumped his things in the middle of the floor and dashed upstairs. Serena bent down to move Henry's things out of the way, and when she stood back up her head started spinning. Her stomach was cramping. She had to get something to eat soon.

Serena walked to the kitchen and flipped open the pizza box from last night. The box was empty; the slices she and Henry left inside had disappeared—along with any hope for a quick and easy dinner.

Well, at least her father was eating something, Serena thought. Maybe he'd made a run to the grocery store, too.

She flipped up the lid of the bread box with a bang, but there was no bread. That ruled out grilled cheese sandwiches, or peanut butter and jelly. She walked over to the refrigerator and yanked open the door, making the jars on the shelf rattle. No hot dogs. Further searching revealed that there were no more frozen hamburger patties, no more macaroni and cheese, and no white rice, spaghetti, spaghetti sauce, or deli meat. The casserole dishes from their friends and neighbors had stopped coming months ago. Serena wanted to scream. What did her father think they were supposed to eat? Did he even think of them at all?

Serena snatched down a box of stale saltine crackers and a jar of peanut butter from the cabinet just as Henry came into the kitchen.

"What's for dinner?" he asked, looking hungrily at the peanut butter in Serena's hand.

"I don't know," Serena said irritably. "Why are you asking me?" But she knew why. Who else was there for him to ask?

Henry's face puckered and she softened her tone. "Where's Dad?" she asked him.

Henry shrugged and reached for one of the cracker sandwiches she had made. Serena grabbed one, too, and they both munched noisily.

"Mmdtno," Henry mumbled.

Serena got up and poured them each a glass of water. After waiting for Henry to take a drink she said, "What?"

"I said I don't know," he answered. Serena noticed a very un-Henry-like edge to his voice.

"You can't find him?" Serena asked after another sip of water.

97

"Didn't look," Henry answered, grabbing another cracker sandwich off the plate.

Serena's eyebrows shot up. Henry always, *always*, looked for their dad after school. That's what Henry did. He came home, dumped his stuff on the floor, and wandered around the house until he found their father so he could talk a mile a minute about his day.

Henry sat quietly while Serena made more cracker sandwiches. She pushed three toward Henry and watched him. Something about him wasn't quite right. And then she realized—he wasn't saying a word. Henry *always* talked. He'd been noisy from the time he came home from the hospital.

"So, what's going on at school?" Serena asked him. Henry shrugged. "Did you get in trouble or something?" Henry shrugged again. "Is that a yes or a no?"

"I don't know," Henry mumbled. He got up from the table.

"Going to look for Dad?" she asked him as he turned to leave the room.

"No," he said, and he walked out.

Serena put her head in her hands. The crackers had helped her stomach, but it would take her head a little while to stop hurting. She thought back over the past week, trying to figure out exactly when Henry had become so quiet. Definitely not Monday or Tuesday, and on Wednesday he'd been normal, too. Thursday he'd been talking about the gerbil and the "hearsal." So something must have happened today.

Eyeing the envelope from Henry's teacher that still lay unopened on the counter, Serena suddenly had a thought. She ripped it open.

Dear Mr. Shaw,

Let me start by first expressing my sympathy for the loss of your wife. Losing a loved one is never easy, but losing a wife and mother can be devastating for a family. Until recently I have been impressed by how Henry has handled this severe life change. However, in the past few weeks, I have noticed that Henry has become increasingly contrary and disruptive in class. As this sort of behavior is quite out of character for your son, I would like to address the matter as quickly as possible, before it becomes a much bigger problem.

I'm hoping this letter will facilitate a face-to-face meeting so that we can discuss an action plan to get Henry's behavior back on track. Please call me at your earliest convenience to set a time for a parent/teacher conference.

Thank you for your prompt attention to this matter.

Sincerely,

Mrs. Duwee

Underneath her signature, the teacher had written her phone number in large numerals so it couldn't be missed.

Serena put the letter down and returned her head to her hands. She tried to think clearly, but her head was pounding so hard that it was difficult to gather her thoughts. Serena had always relied on Henry to raise her father's spirits, and her own, too. Sometimes Henry was the only thing that could make her father smile. Henry could be a little annoying, but even Serena had to admit that mostly, he was an angel. A sweet, happy little boy.

But now Serena was certain that even though he hadn't said anything, Henry could tell how sad and out of it their dad was. First their mom disappeared forever, and now their dad was starting to fade away, too. Their father's depression was defining their lives, surrounding them, and it felt like there was nothing she could do to stop it.

Serena pulled her head out of her hands. Well, the first thing she had to do was figure out dinner.

"Okay," she said to the empty kitchen. "There's no food in the house. So that means we have to order out. We had pizza last night, and it's been at least eight days since we had Chinese food. So Chinese it is."

The appliances around her were silent. "Good," Serena told them. "We agree."

Serena sang as she surveyed the Chinese menu. *"Have an egg roll, Mr. Goldstone, have a napkin, have a chopstick, have a chair.*" There were only two things that Henry ever ate—crab-cheese wontons and egg rolls.

Serena picked up the phone to dial, but noticed the staccato beeps indicating that they had new messages. She'd never worried about getting phone messages before. Once Kat had left eleven messages in one night after another crush gone bad, and Serena's mother had made it embarrassingly clear to all her friends that only people who paid their own phone bills were eligible to leave messages.

Serena found the cheat sheet for picking up messages in the junk drawer and went through the steps.

"You have twenty-four new messages," the voice informed her.

Twenty-four! Twenty-four? When was the last time her father had checked the machine?

"First message. Monday, December 27, 9:18 a.m.," the voice informed her.

The twenty-seventh? That was over three weeks ago! Just after December 26—her mother's birthday. Which, now that Serena thought about it, was right around the time her father had started zoning out.

At first, there were just a couple of things that didn't seem quite right, like not laughing at Henry's lame jokes, or forgetting to ask how Serena's day at school had been. But then he began spending more and more time in his office, without appearing to do any work. Then he would hardly leave the house, and barely got the laundry and grocery shopping done. After that he started wearing his pajamas and crying all the time. And now he was totally useless.

Serena started. The voice on the machine was telling her to save or delete the current message, or to press star for more options. Serena grabbed a piece of scrap paper and a pen, sat at the kitchen table, and punched the star.

Fifteen minutes and a full sheet of messages later, Serena knew that her father had gotten eight messages from his agent and missed out on four illustration jobs because he hadn't called her back. There had been four calls from Mrs. Duwee, and four messages from Serena's school, informing him that she'd skipped her sixth-period class three times a few weeks back. Serena was glad he'd missed those at least. There were three calls from his friends, just checking in. And five calls from her uncle Peter.

Message one: "Yo, boy! Sorry I haven't called. The firm's got me traveling so much I don't know what country I'm in half the time. Get in touch with a brother. Let me know what's going on. Later!"

Message two: "Hey, Black man, can't return a brother's phone call? I gotta tell you about my new girl, Janiece! Hit a brother's digits back!"

Message three: "Okay, look, I'm about to take this mess personally. You already missed out on meeting Janiece.

She's yesterday's news. Look, I'm back in the States for at least this weekend. Let's take the kids out someplace. I know they're missing their fav uncle. Call me so we can set it up."

Message four: "Yo, man, I know I said we need to get together this weekend, but I met me this fine lady. She's only in town for the weekend, and since you ain't even called a brother back nohow, I'm gonna show her the town. Tell Serena and Henry I'll make it up to them. Ask if cash still works! Give 'em hugs from me. Later!"

The last message was dated today, just a few hours before school had ended.

"Hey, man, got your text, and gotta say it freaked me out a little. I know you miss Vivian. I miss her, too, and she wasn't hardly even nice to me half the time. Seriously, though, you got Serena and Henry, don't forget that. You have to lift yourself out of that funk for their sake. I'm out for at least a week, heading to Prague. Sitting at the airport as we speak, but you can still e-mail me, my phone service is a little iffy over there, but feel free to text or call me, whenever. Anytime. Keep your head up! Peace. I'll be in touch as soon as I'm back in the U.S."

Uncle Peter's last message made Serena a little nervous. After hanging up, Serena neatly rewrote all the messages on a clean sheet of paper. Knocking on her father's bedroom door, she peeked into the dark room. She heard a soft snore coming from the bed.

Watching him sleep, Serena was torn between wanting to shake her father awake and hoping that a good night's rest would jog him out of his funk. Her mother had always told her and Henry to be quiet and to leave their father alone when he was in his "moods." And he'd always seemed to get better eventually. So maybe if Serena did what her mother used to do, everything would be okay.

Tiptoeing inside the room, she laid the paper on his nightstand and walked away, quietly shutting the door behind her. She hoped her father would actually read it.

11

"Serena! Serena!"

Serena woke up to Henry shaking her and calling her name. She groaned and pushed his hand off her shoulder. She'd been asleep with no dreams and Henry had ruined it.

"Go away, Henry," she mumbled, pulling the covers up to her neck. "It's Saturday. Go watch cartoons or something."

"But I'm hungry," Henry whined. "Get up." He tugged Serena's blankets off her. "Get up, now."

The tone of Henry's voice made Serena open her eyes and glare at him.

"Boy, you better watch how you talk to me," she warned. "Go away. I'm tired."

"But I'm hungry," Henry repeated. "There's not any cereal or anything." Serena felt the bed give as Henry sat down. "Go finish the wontons from last night," she said.

She rolled over, turning her back to him, and burrowed deeper under her covers.

"I already did," Henry answered. "There were only two left. I'm still hungry."

Serena tried to relax, willing herself to go back to sleep, but Henry wouldn't budge. He sat next to her silently.

It was his silence that lured Serena out from under her covers. Flipping them back, she rolled over to look at him. Tears were streaming down his face.

"Whoa, dude," Serena said, sitting up. "Look, how about we walk down to the café and get some bagels and hot chocolate for breakfast. You know, like we used to?"

Henry nodded silently, but the tears kept rolling down his cheeks.

A wave of helplessness washed over Serena. "Henry, what is it? What's the matter?" she asked, pulling him closer. He sank against her.

Henry shrugged.

"If nothing is wrong, then why are you crying? Are you that hungry?"

He responded with another forlorn lift of his shoulders.

Serena thought for a minute. What would her mother do? Suddenly she remembered.

She made a fist and very gently tapped Henry on his chest, where his heart was.

The briefest of smiles touched Henry's lips. "Yes?" he said softly.

Serena sang to him:

"Knock, knock. It's me,
I love you, yes I do!
You seem sad,
and just a little blue.
What's laying heavy in your heart?
Please tell me something true!"

"I hate school," Henry said after a moment.

Serena's insides clenched. Henry had always had good things to say about school before. This wasn't a good sign. Not at all.

"Why?" she asked him.

"Because I don't have no friends," he answered, his eyes filling with tears again.

"What do you mean?" Serena asked. She thought about all the times she'd picked him up from school. There were always tons of kids wanting to tell Henry one last thing, or asking him to come over. "I thought you had a ton of friends in your class," she said.

Henry shook his head forlornly. "No one likes me anymore, 'cause I've got the dead mommy cooties, and those are the worst cooties to have. Everyone in my class says so."

Serena immediately lost her cool. "What! What kind of crap is that?" she asked angrily.

"Well, it's true," Henry insisted. "Mommy is dead and now I have the dead mommy cooties and people don't want to be near me 'cause they might get them, too."

Serena opened her mouth but said nothing. What was she supposed to say to that? If their father was his regular brown self instead of blue, he'd come in and comfort Henry. He'd take him off to his office, and together they would draw out the problem. Then they'd crumple up the pictures and throw them away, and spend time drawing pictures of how life was supposed to be. That tack always worked like a charm on Henry.

But Serena's father did not magically appear.

"Um," Serena said, doing her best to solve the problem on her own. "Have you told your teacher about these cooties?"

Henry shook his head. "She says cooties are make-believe and not to let it bother me. I don't think grown-ups know too much about cooties. Malik says it's dangerous to play with me, and now no one will."

Serena felt an electric surge of fury. That freakin' brat Malik.

"There's no such thing as cooties, Henry," she said firmly.

Henry only shook his head harder. "Yeah so. There's lots of different kind of cooties. Girl cooties, boy cooties, dead mommy cooties." His face was adamant.

Serena thought for a minute. "Well, if there are dead mommy cooties, there must be dead daddy cooties, too, right?"

Henry seemed to be thinking about this possibility. "Yeah, I guess so," he said.

"And if there are dead daddy cooties, there are dead grandma cooties, too," Serena went on. "Which means that Malik has them." She knew for a fact that Malik's grandmother had died two years ago, because after the funeral, her mother had made his family a dish of chicken enchiladas. Serena had gotten in trouble for eating some before her mother could take it over to them. "So you'd better warn everyone about playing with Malik, too, or they might catch the dead grandma cooties. And those are just as bad as the dead mommy cooties ones."

She could see the wheels in Henry's head turning. He nodded. "Yeah, I gotta tell them." But he still looked upset. "Cooties are catchy, you know," he said. "Malik said that if the other kids don't want their moms to die then they better not get too close to me."

"Okay. So, if you're a boy and you play with a girl, do you get girl cooties and become one?" Serena asked.

"No, that's stupid," Henry told her, rolling his eyes at Serena's clear lack of cootie knowledge. "Boys can play with girls and girls can play with boys, except girls don't play fun games."

"So cooties aren't really dangerous then," Serena said.

"I mean, either you can catch cooties or you can't." She reached over and started poking Henry playfully. "Oh, no, I've got boy cooties! I'm becoming a stinky boy! I want to burp and pee standing up!" She poked Henry in all his ticklish places, until he began to giggle.

"Ew, you're nasty, Serena," he said, giggling madly. "And you're still a stinky girl!"

"Wow, I guess I *am* still a girl!" she said, her voice full of amazement. "Well, let's see if I can give you some girl cooties!"

She pounced on Henry, tickling him until he was out of breath. She stopped and took his face in her hand, turning it this way and that. "Do you feel like playing dolls with me? Maybe you'd like to borrow one of my dresses! I can braid your hair and put in some ribbons!" She pawed through his hair and lifted up his arm and looked carefully at his armpit. She made a super sad face and said, "Wow, I was *sure* I'd have a little sister after I gave you all those girl cooties. But you're still a stinky little boy!"

Henry giggled. "I'm not stinky."

"Well, then," Serena told him. "If you didn't get my girl cooties I guess that means they aren't catchy after all. You'd better tell everyone at school. Tell them we did research! Now get out of my room, go get dressed, and let's go get some hot chocolate."

Henry reached over and gave Serena a big hug. "I'm so

hungry I could eat a whole herd of bears!" he said as he trotted out of the room.

As Serena watched Henry leave, an intense relief swept over her. If only all their other problems were as easily solved.

SITTING AT THE TINY TABLE NEAR THE WINDOWS IN THE coffee shop, Serena watched her brother sip his hot chocolate and eat his bagel and half of hers, all the while talking a mile a minute. She was happy that he seemed to be back to his old self again. Still, her stomach was full of butterflies. Once they got home, Serena was going to have to find her father and drag him out of the house to the grocery store. They'd probably have to go to the bank, too. Serena knew for a fact that he'd gotten a check for the illustrations he'd turned in last month, and she'd seen the huge settlement check from the trucking company sitting next to it in the mail basket in the front hall. It had come the same week as her mother's birthday, like some sort of morbid birthday gift. As if the trucking company was saying, "So sorry our driver killed your mom, but each year we'll send this check to make you feel better!" Who would have ever thought that thousands of dollars could make a person feel so sad?

The bell over the coffee shop door jingled for what seemed like the hundredth time since they'd gotten there.

On Saturday mornings, the café was *the* place to be, and usually Serena sat facing the door, looking to see who else would show up. Today, though, she was too tired to care. It wasn't until Henry called out, "Hi, *amigo*!" and waved his arm, knocking the remains of her hot chocolate all over the table, that she even looked up.

"Smooth move, Ex-Lax!" she snapped, leaping out of her seat to avoid the dripping chocolate.

"Este debe ser mi día afortunado!" a familiar voice called out. *"Pensé en ti anoche!"*

There was Elijah, heading over to their table.

"Buenos días, mi estrella hermosa," he said, grabbing some napkins to help her finish cleaning the spill.

"Yeah," muttered Serena. *"Buenos días, llore rociado* to you, too."

Elijah burst out laughing at her nonsensical Spanish. "What are you guys doing here?" He pulled up a chair and sat down at their table.

Serena rolled her eyes. "We're taking a swim, what do you think we're doing?"

Elijah laughed again and Serena smiled at him.

"You here alone?" she asked.

"Yeah, my mom wanted a couple dozen bagels for this thing she's having at the house and I got sent to fetch them for her."

"Fetch them, eh?" Serena said. She reached over and

petted him on the head. "Ohh, what a good boy you are! Yes, you are!"

Elijah grinned and started panting, and then he suddenly grabbed her hand and licked it.

"Oh, eww!" Serena shrieked. She wiped the back of her hand on her jeans and flicked him in the shoulder. "That is so gross, you freak."

Henry and Elijah laughed.

"*Deliciosa*," Elijah said, giving her a wink.

Serena glared at him for as long as she could before breaking into a grin. "Yeah, whatever. I swear I'm going to tell our teacher that you speak Spanish like a native if you don't stop. Well, since pinhead over there ate my bagel, then spilled my drink, I think it's time we be headed home."

"Oh, big plans for today, Serena Star?" Elijah asked her.

"I need to go to the grocery store and study my lines," she said, reaching for her coat. "My life is very exciting. Try not to be jealous."

The door jingled again. Glancing over, Serena saw Kat, Nikka, and two boys strolling in, laughing and talking loudly. The boys were serious hotties. They had to be Marcus and what's-his-name. Serena felt her insides tighten with jealousy. Kat noticed Serena and waved, heading over to her with what's-his-name behind her. "Yo, girlie! What up? What you doing here?" she said, her voice slightly higher than usual with excitement.

"Henry and I were getting breakfast," Serena answered. Nikka was strutting over coolly, Marcus in tow. Serena suppressed a grimace. Nikka thought she was so cute. "Don't tell me that you guys are *still* on your date from last night?"

Kat giggled hysterically. What's-his-name grinned. "Girl, naw. You know my folks wouldn't even allow that. We just had such a bomb time last night we couldn't wait to hook up again!"

What's-his-name didn't look much older than Kat. He was probably only a freshman, which made Serena feel a little bit better, but not much. Nikka and Kat were having dates, real live dates, with high school guys, while Serena was feeding her annoying little brother and getting ready to go grocery shopping with her crazy dad. *So* not fair.

She reached out her hand to what's-his-name. "Hi, I'm Serena," she said.

"Ian," he said, shaking her hand limply.

Marcus greeted her, too, when he and Nikka reached them. "I'm Marcus. What up?" He turned to Nikka. "What do you want?"

"Vanilla crème frappe," she said, batting her eyelashes at him. Serena suppressed a groan.

Marcus and Ian went off to get the drinks for Nikka

and Kat. Serena wished there was someone to get *her* a drink. Some cute high school boy.

"Oh, by the way," she told her friends, ignoring her pangs of envy, "thanks for picking up Henry yesterday. I meant to call you guys last night to thank you. It was such a life-saver. I was hoping maybe—"

"Yeah, well, just don't think we'll be doing it again," Nikka interrupted. "We'll probably be meeting Marcus and Ian after school from now on."

Serena turned to Kat, but she was staring moony-eyed over at Ian, who was leaning against the counter, staring moony-eyed right back at her.

Serena's heart actually hurt. Even Kat didn't have her back.

"Oh, sure, yeah," Serena said, her voice full of fake cheer. "No worries, girlies."

"Okay, well, we'll talk later, okay?" Kat said.

"Yeah, talk with ya later," Serena answered.

Kat and Nikka hurried off to join their new boy-friends, settling in a booth in the back. They only took up half the booth, with Kat and Nikka practically sitting on the boys' laps.

"You okay?"

Elijah waved his hand in front of Serena's face.

"Huh? Oh, yeah, sure," Serena answered.

"I don't believe you," Elijah replied. He quirked an eyebrow and waited for her to say something.

115

She heaved a big sigh. "I was hoping that Kat and Nikka would pick Henry up from school for me until after the play ended, but, fine, whatever." She waved her hand toward the booth where the couples sat. "They clearly have other things to do. Now I have to tell Mr. Hobbs I'll be late to rehearsal every single day." Serena was feeling overwhelmed. "Or maybe I should just quit the stupid play. It's becoming too complicated anyway."

"I'll do it," Elijah said.

"Yippee!" Henry shouted from the table.

"But you have the sets to finish," Serena told Elijah. "It's bad enough to have Henry running around every single rehearsal. I don't think Mr. Hobbs would like it if we don't have any sets because you're chasing after him all the time."

"First of all, Henry isn't running around at rehearsals, he's working with me and the rest of the crew. And he's probably the best up there. Well, besides me—right, little man? And secondly, I'm totally on schedule, due to my fantastic organizational skills. So really, it's not a problem."

Henry stuck out his bottom lip and looked at her with his "please, please, pretty please" face.

"Well, okay," she said to Elijah. "I mean, if you don't mind. It would be a huge help. And I really could use some help right now," she added, more to herself than to anyone else.

"Hey, no problem," Elijah said. Henry began bouncing around with joy. "Henry's my homie, ain't that right, little man?"

Serena laughed as she put on her coat. "Good God," she said, trying to herd Henry toward the door. "At this point I'm totally in debt to you." Elijah opened his mouth but Serena cut him off before he could say anything. "Boy, I swear if you say something in Spanish I will beat you," she warned.

Elijah laughed. "No worries," he said. "I like having you in debt to me." Then, with a wink, he turned and headed to the counter to buy his bagels.

As he walked away, Serena could have sworn she saw a halo floating over his head.

12

As Henry rambled and chatted nonstop the entire way home, Serena realized she was beginning to feel better. She had already solved two problems this morning. Things were looking up.

"Okay, Henry," she said when they reached the house. "How about you make a grocery list for us while I go get Daddy?"

"Okay!" Henry ran off to the kitchen and Serena went in search of their father. He wasn't in his bedroom, and the office was empty, too. On his desk was a plate with the leftover pizza from Thursday night. There were a couple of bites taken from one of the pieces, but the other slice had been left untouched and was now dried-up and crusty. Serena snatched up the plate, flicked off the lights, slammed the door, and headed back upstairs. She could have given that pizza to Henry last night for dinner, instead of giving herself brain damage trying to figure out what else to eat. She threw away the dried-up pizza and put the dirty dish into the dishwasher.

Henry was writing his grocery list at the kitchen table. Serena peeked over his shoulder.

ice cream
cereal
milk
bread
spagtii
chees
ornage jucie
hot dogs
forzen pizza
meat
macaroane and chees
crackers
egg

"Good job, Henry," she said, patting him on the back even as she grimaced at his atrocious spelling. She hoped it was normal for a second grader to spell like that. "You done yet?" she asked.

"I think so," he answered.

Serena went back to looking for their father. Where could he have gone? And why hadn't he left a note?

Of course, *she* hadn't left a note when they went to the café.

That was it! Serena realized. Her father must have noticed they were missing and gone to look for them. She went out to the garage to see if his car was still there.

The garage light was on. Serena yanked open the door and peered inside.

Her heart dropped. Both cars were still parked in the garage. She was about to shut the door when she saw him, seated in her mother's car—or rather, the car that her mother used to drive. He looked like he was still in his pajamas, and he had something on his lap.

"Dad!" she called. "What are you doing out here? It's cold." She wound her way over to the car.

Her father looked up at her. He opened the car door. "Hey, baby," he said softly.

"What's that?" she asked, pointing to the book in his lap. "What are you doing?"

"Oh, this?" he said. "This is our wedding album. I was looking at it."

"In the garage?" Serena asked. "In the car?"

Her father gave a small chuckle. "Yeah, crazy, I know. It's just that the car, well, it still smells a little like her. I like to sit in here sometimes and . . . You needed me?"

Serena wanted to scream. Did she *need* him? What kind of stupid question was that? Of course she needed him!

Henry needed him! He was their father, for crying out loud!

"Yeah, Dad," she snapped. "I freakin' need you." She waited for a reprimand but got none. "We have no food, and I've used up all the money in your wallet. We gotta go to the bank and to the grocery store. Like now. Go get dressed."

Her father heaved a huge sigh. "Oh, baby, how about I go to the store tomorrow, or maybe Monday?" He rubbed his hand across his cheek, which sounded like sandpaper. He seriously needed a shave.

"No, Daddy," Serena told him. "We have no bread, no milk, no cereal, no hot dogs, no juice, no frozen hamburger patties, no nothing! We need to go to the grocery store *today*. Not tomorrow, not the next day, today! If we run out of toilet paper I will lose it for real."

"Fine," he said with a groan. "I'll drive you to the store."

Serena waited as her father got out of the car. "Dad," she said, "aren't you going to take the picture album?"

"Oh," he replied. "It's fine there. I'll, um . . . it's okay where it is."

Serena sighed. It was so hard to be mad at her father, when she understood so well what he was doing. She did it, too—trying to hold on to little things to remember her mother. Every time she watched an old movie her mom had enjoyed, or sang a song from some old 1940s musical, she could feel her mother's presence. So Serena knew why her father needed to look at pictures. And she knew he'd be back as soon as he could, sitting in her mother's old car, smelling the last scent of her and flipping through their wedding album. But even though she understood, she still hated him for it.

AFTER GOING TO THE DRIVE-THROUGH ATM AT THE BANK, her father stuffed the wad of cash in his wallet, drove across the street to the grocery store, and handed Serena his credit card. Then he sat in the car while she and Henry did the grocery shopping.

A year ago, Serena would have loved to be in charge of buying the food for the house. Now, though, she knew that she couldn't just buy the junk food she wanted. There were things, necessities, that had to be purchased—stuff that Henry hadn't written on his list, like dryer sheets, dishwasher soap, and toilet paper. When she and Henry had finished shopping and pushed the heavy cart out to the parking lot, their father didn't even get out to help them load the groceries into the car.

By the time she and Henry had unloaded the groceries and put them away, Serena felt exhausted, but it was their father who walked slowly up to his bedroom as if he had done all the work. Serena didn't have the energy to go after him to talk about the letter from Henry's teacher. She didn't even feel like studying her lines. All she wanted to do was veg out, and maybe have some fun for a change. She wondered if Kat and Nikka were around. It'd been a while since they'd all hung out together.

"Hey, girlie, what up?" Serena said as soon as Kat had picked up the phone. She made herself comfortable on the couch. "You have got to come over and tell me about Ian. Bring a movie, spend the night, or something!"

"Hey, I'm on the other line with him right now," Kat answered. "I'll call you back, 'kay?"

"Oh, sure," Serena said, trying to ignore the hurt she felt. "I'll be here."

Kat hung up without saying goodbye. Serena started to dial Nikka's number but found she wasn't in the mood to deal with her superior attitude. Instead, she sat holding the phone, feeling alone and friendless. The idea of calling Candy came to mind, but she didn't want to talk about the play—or their dead mothers. She wanted a fun, nonserious conversation. The kind of conversation that normal seventh graders got to have.

"Serena, is it dinnertime yet?" Henry asked, plopping down on the couch beside her.

Serena sighed. "Yeah. Let's have that frozen lasagna we got today, and the garlic bread."

Henry let out a cheer. "Yeah! Can I help cook it?"

Serena smiled despite her funky mood. At least Henry was back to his old self again. She nodded and stood up.

As she was putting the phone back on the cradle it rang. Kat!

"Hello?" she said happily.

"Buenas noches, mi amor." Definitely not Kat.

"Elijah? What are you calling for?" Serena said.

"Dang, I thought you'd be thrilled to hear from me," Elijah said.

"I'm just surprised to hear from you. Oh, God, is this about one of those favors I owe you?"

Elijah laughed. "Well, yes, I guess it is."

"I don't have a bunch of money, so don't trip!" Serena said. Her stomach fluttered. "Okay, so, what is it?"

"Don't sound so freaked out," Elijah said. "I just need to know what section five is for our social studies project proposal."

"Huh?" Serena replied. "What are you talking about?"

"The proposal for our social studies project. It's due Monday. The final project is due, um, sometime, like, in a few weeks, remember?"

"Crap, crap, crap!" Serena shouted. She'd totally forgotten about that stupid social studies project.

"Problem, Serena Star?" Elijah said, before breaking out laughing at her.

"Oh, shut up," Serena muttered. "Hold on, let me go and get the paper."

Serena tossed the phone on the couch, ran up to her room, and dug through her backpack. She pulled out her social studies folder and flipped through the papers. Nothing. She looked in her English, math, Spanish, and even her chorus music folders. Nothing. Finally, after dumping out her entire backpack on her bed, she found the directions, crumpled up in the bottom of her bag.

Section five was preparing an outline of the project.

"Thanks, Serena," Elijah said. "*Yo*—"

"Don't you dare start speaking Spanish," Serena warned him.

He laughed. "So what are you doing this fine evening?"

"Well, thanks to you, I'm stressing about that darn social studies proposal. What about you? In English, please."

"Thinking of you," he answered.

"Yeah, whatever," Serena said. "You've always got jokes."

"Who's joking?"

Serena opened her mouth, getting ready to give him a smart comment, but stopped herself.

"Um, you?" she asked softly. "You're joking?" She could feel her face getting warmer and warmer.

"Nope, not joking. Quite serious. I'm an artist, after all. We are known for being very serious."

"I thought artists were known for being crazy. You know, chopping off ears and stuff," Serena said.

"Oh, there are a few things, people, I'm crazy about," Elijah replied. "But speaking of crazy artists, I'm doing my project on the artists of Renaissance Europe."

"Oh, were they really crazy? That'd be interesting to

write about." Serena's cheeks were beginning to feel cooler now that they had veered back into a more normal conversation. Maybe she'd misunderstood the whole "thinking of you" comment.

"I have no clue. I just came up with my subject today. Besides, we don't need to know names and stuff until, oh, what is the deadline for note cards?"

Serena consulted the paper.

"Next week, Friday," she answered. "Crap!"

"What?"

"Oh, this stupid project is due the same week of the play! Like I need something like this to take up my time. Why does she have to spread out the project like that, anyway, and torture us week after week after week? What kind of teacher does that?"

"Yeah, there's nothing more annoying than education taking time away from all the fun stuff, right?"

"Ain't that the truth," Serena answered.

Elijah laughed. "You're a trip, but I like you."

"Okay, well, I guess I better go figure out what I'm going to do for this social studies project."

"Yep, take it easy, Serena Star."

"Right back atcha, van Gogh," Serena said before hanging up. Once she was sure the line was disconnected, she added, "And I like you, too."

13

The rest of Serena's weekend was spent preparing meals for Henry and herself, studying her lines, and writing her social studies proposal. She had finally decided to write about the great African civilizations of Ghana, Mali, and Songhay. She figured that the subject might not be so terrible. In fact, if the project hadn't been due on the same day as opening night, Serena might have actually been into it. But as it was, it seemed like another brick on the load of her life.

On Sunday evening, after putting Henry to bed, Serena knocked tentatively on her father's bedroom door.

There was a muffled response. Serena opened the door and peered into the gloom.

"Daddy?"

"Yes, Serena?" her father said with a sigh.

Serena gritted her teeth at her father's tone. "Um, did you happen to read that letter from Henry's teacher that I left on the counter for you?"

"No, leave it there. I'll read it later."

"No, Daddy, you need to read it now," Serena said. She stepped into the room and flicked on the light. Her father moaned and threw an arm over his eyes.

"It's probably a permission slip. Just sign my name, will you?"

"It's not a permission slip, Dad," Serena snapped. She tossed the letter onto the bed. "It's about Henry. His teacher's worried about his behavior."

"His behavior?" muttered her father. "Behavior problems aren't like him."

"Gee, Dad, ya think? So you gotta call his teacher in the morning. Get it all worked out. Right?"

Her father sat on the bed and stared at the letter without reading it.

"Right, Dad?" Serena repeated.

"I don't know if I can do this," he said quietly.

"Do what? What's the big deal? Call the teacher, tell her that you'll talk to Henry. Done deal."

"There's just too much to do," her father said. "I'm so sad. I always feel so tired. Poor Henry, I bet he's sad and tired, too."

"Yeah, we are all sad and tired, Dad," Serena told him. "But stuff still has to get done. You can't just stop."

"Don't you want it all to end sometimes?" her father said. "Don't you wish you could just go to sleep, and stay that way?"

"Yeah, well, it doesn't work like that, does it?" Serena said. "You gotta keep moving. Get out of bed. Take a shower, that's always a good start."

Like a defiant child, her father tossed the letter on the bed and crawled under the covers.

"Turn out the light when you leave, Serena."

"You *will* call the teacher, right?" Serena asked him again. She was trying not to panic. She'd never seen her father act quite like this before. When he didn't answer, she went to the bed and shook him. "Daddy, you will call Henry's teacher tomorrow morning, right? Her phone number is right there at the bottom of the letter."

"The light, Serena," was all he said.

Serena marched over, turned off the light, and slammed the door behind her.

Once outside his room, she slid down the wall and pulled her knees to her chest. Through the door she could hear her father sobbing. The more he cried, the more she hated his guts.

EARLY MONDAY MORNING IT WAS ALL SERENA COULD DO to get out of bed. She knew that her bad night of sleep was because of her father's behavior. She'd watched an old movie last night, *Harvey*, and they had carted this nice old guy off to the nuthouse. Of course, he was talking to an invisible rabbit, but still. If Henry's teacher kept calling their father and getting no answer, who knew what might happen? Humming to herself, Serena hugged her knees close to her body and rocked back and forth in bed until an idea popped into her head.

Serena sat down at the computer and began to type.

Dear Mrs. Duwee,

I am sorry I haven't returned your calls. My doctor gave me strict orders not to talk to anyone, due to my strained vocal cords. I'm sorry to hear about Henry's behavior. He told me that Malik Jackson was saying mean things about him to the other students. Maybe you could look into this. I'm sure that you understand how sad my little boy is about the death of my wife and I hope you will give him a break. I'm sure he will be much better behaved really soon.

Thank you,
Michael D. Shaw

She printed the letter, signed it with a fair imitation of her father's artistic scrawl, and stuffed it into an envelope before putting it into Henry's backpack. If by some miracle her father did actually call the teacher, he would just have to figure out a way to explain the letter himself. That would serve him right.

Forging the letter had taken more time than Serena

expected, and she found herself running from Henry's school in a sprint to get to first period on time. After ten tardies she'd get a lower math grade, and Serena knew she was already dancing close to the edge.

After plopping into her seat at the last possible moment, Serena tried her hardest to concentrate on the lesson. But her mind, which was never inclined to focus on math anyway, refused to contemplate the dubious merits of algebra. Instead it wandered from Henry to her father to the play before stopping, much to her surprise, on Elijah.

Serena thought about the conversation they'd had on Saturday night and felt her stomach fill with butterflies. Uh-oh. She knew that feeling.

"Miss Shaw?"

With effort Serena zoned back into class and found the teacher and the class staring at her.

"Um, could you repeat the question?" she asked sheepishly.

Her algebra teacher shook her head, while around her a few students tittered. "I asked what you got for problem 14."

"Oh, yeah, um, $x = 72$," Serena answered quickly, looking down at her homework.

"That's correct," said Mrs. Grayson.

"Whoa, for real?" Serena asked, before clamping a

hand over her mouth. The class and Mrs. Grayson laughed.

SERENA FELT NERVOUS HEADING TO SPANISH. SHE HADN'T heard from Elijah since Saturday, so she really didn't know what to expect when she saw him in class.

Elijah was leaning against the wall outside the door. He seemed to be waiting for her.

"Serena Star, what up?" he asked, walking with her into the classroom.

"Not a thing. And you?" Serena tried to sound casual, but the butterflies of doom had returned to her stomach, confirming her earlier suspicion. She was totally crushing on Elijah.

"You finish the proposal?" he asked as he slid into the chair next to her.

"Yeah, thanks to you," she said. "I owe . . ." She stopped herself just in time and made a big show of pinching her mouth together.

Elijah laughed. "Girl, you're creating quite a bill with me."

"I don't think it counts," Serena said, grinning at him. "I told you about section five, so that cancels it out."

Elijah chuckled at her. "Yeah, all right, whatever. Did you remember to tell Henry's teacher I'll be picking him up after school from now on?"

Serena's mouth dropped open, but at that moment the

teacher called the class to order and she couldn't reply. Elijah started snickering, and all Serena could do was stick her tongue out at him.

"You know, I may start charging you," the school secretary joked when Serena came in at lunchtime and headed for the phone. "Make a little spending money on the side."

"Yeah, I know, right?" Serena said. She felt unexplainably happy and giddy. She didn't even mind when she got to the lunchroom and discovered that Kat and Nikka had ditched again without inviting her. What did she care? Kat hadn't even bothered to call her back last weekend. While Serena was looking around for a place to sit, she saw Candy and Elijah waving her over to join them. *Since when do they eat together?* Serena thought, shocked by an electric zing of jealousy. But then she noticed that the rest of the table was filled with *Wiz* people, and a feeling of relief swept over her. She headed toward the table.

Serena spent the lunch period laughing and talking with the rest of the cast and crew about the play and all the gossip and drama that had been going on backstage. When the subject of play hookups started, Serena felt her face grow hot. She forced herself not to look over at Elijah, even though he kept nudging her foot under the table.

The rest of the day flew by and finally it was time for rehearsal.

The cast and crew had just settled down to work when Mr. Hobbs looked around and asked, "Where is my artistic director? Don't tell me he's flaked out on me so soon."

Serena walked over to him. "It's my fault he's late, Mr. Hobbs, but I promise he'll be here soon."

Mr. Hobbs cocked an eyebrow at her, but just then Elijah and Henry burst through the door, playing what appeared to be a game of tag.

Henry sprinted down the aisle, squealing with glee.

"Hi, Serena!" he cried. He flew into her and gave her a big hug. Then, without another word, he marched up the stairs, dropped his backpack with an echoing bang, and started arranging the paints.

Elijah trotted down the aisle, winking at Serena and tipping his baseball cap to Mr. Hobbs, and joined Henry on the stage.

Mr. Hobbs turned to Serena. "So your brother is *still* helping out with the sets, huh?" he asked. Serena nodded, and Mr. Hobbs looked at her uneasily. "I don't know about that, Serena. Having him paint the base coats was fine. But this performance will be under the microscope! Our set has to look perfect, and preschool art isn't the look I'd like to shoot for."

Serena's heart sank. "He's in second grade," she mumbled feebly.

"Perhaps your father could arrange his schedule for the next few weeks so that your brother won't have to come here every afternoon. Or is there something going on at home I should know about?"

Serena's mouth dropped open. She couldn't think of any words to say.

"Yo! Excuse me, Mr. Hobbs!" Elijah called from up on the stage. "Could you come check this out, please?"

Both Mr. Hobbs and Serena turned toward him.

"Can y'all come up here for a sec and peep this?"

Serena and Mr. Hobbs climbed up the steps and met Elijah center stage.

"Okay, so I've got this idea, right? For the tornado. I wanted to somehow give it a feeling of motion, so we got this supersized roll of paper, and put it on two big sticks, like one of those old-time scrolls. So, during the tornado sequence we roll out the paper and it looks like the wind is blowing. I asked my homeboy Henry here to start making the clouds and stuff and look what he did."

Elijah signaled to a couple of the backstage crew, who picked up the roll of paper and spread it out the length of the stage. Gray, ominous storm clouds were painted across it. As they slowly turned the roll, the paper moved from one spindle to the other, and the clouds grew darker and stormier. Serena watched in wonder. Suddenly the clouds began to swirl, and she could actually see items being pulled up into the tornado as the paper was turned.

"Outstanding!" Mr. Hobbs shouted. "Unbelievable job, Elijah!"

"That was incredible," Serena agreed, grinning at him.

"Yeah, it is incredible," Elijah said, "but I barely painted any of it." He pointed over to Henry. "My boy over there did it."

Henry, who hadn't stopped his painting despite all the talking around him, continued to work, oblivious to the fact that the three of them were looking in his direction.

"Naw," Serena said, turning back to Elijah. "You got jokes."

Elijah shook his head. "I've been focusing on the poppy field, trying to give it some depth with different shades of crimson and different-size flowers, so it's not just a boring sea of red. So I told my man Henry to go ahead and start on the tornado. I showed him a couple of techniques to make the clouds darker, and he totally vibed on it. Anyway, I scoped y'all's discussion and thought that you should see my boy's skills before you kicked him to the curb. On the serious tip, he's like way better than people in my art class. It's mad crazy how good he is, especially for a little kid."

Mr. Hobbs shook his head in awe, looking from Henry back to Elijah. "I've seen enough, and I don't need to see any more. Carry on!"

As Mr. Hobbs strode off the stage, Serena turned to Elijah and opened her mouth.

"Ha! Don't even say it!" Elijah said with a laugh. "Believe me, I'm keeping a tally."

"Yeah, well, that last one was worth at least ten," Serena told him. "Thank you." She gave him a heartfelt smile, but what she really wanted to do was grab him by his T-shirt, pull him close, and kiss him. Right there, in front of everybody.

"*Todo para ti*," he replied with a grin.

Serena rolled her eyes so he'd know that she didn't appreciate the Spanish, but as she trotted down the stage steps to take her place by the Scarecrow and Tin Man to practice the harmony for "Ease on Down the Road," she was stunned to realize she had actually understood what Elijah had just said.

"Anything for you."

AFTER REHEARSAL, SERENA AND HENRY CAME HOME TO their dark, quiet house. Henry dropped his things in his usual, totally-in-the-way, middle-of-the-floor spot, but rather than search out their father, he headed straight to the kitchen. Serena followed him and took out some frozen pot pies and nuked them in the microwave. Then she made Henry go wash his hands while she sliced some bread and picked out the wilted pieces of lettuce from the previous night's salad.

Sliding Henry's plate in front of him, she asked, "So how was school today? Any cootie problems?"

"Huh?" Henry mumbled through a mouthful of bread.

"You know, the cootie problem you had last week?"

Henry scrunched his face as if he was trying to figure out what she was talking about.

"Remember? You and—" Serena stopped herself. Why remind him? "Never mind." Serena wished she could forget bad things so quickly.

For a few minutes the only sounds in the kitchen were the crunching of lettuce and swallowing of chicken pot pie. Then Henry said, "Serena? When is Daddy going to be over the blue? My colds never last this long. Why is his taking so long?"

Serena's stomach twisted into a knot. "Stop talking with your mouth full," she snapped at him. Why was he asking her anyway? How was she supposed to know? Why didn't he go ask their father? She took a big bite of her pie so all the nasty words that had popped into her head wouldn't come out of her mouth.

Henry finished his bite, took a swallow of his drink, and then said, "Have you given Daddy any soup? My teacher says that chicken soup makes you feel better. You should give him some chicken soup."

Serena got up from the table and dumped her remaining food into the sink without answering.

"Or maybe if you—"

The rest of Henry's sentence was drowned out by the garbage disposal that Serena had flicked on. She watched the rest of her dinner go down the drain, trying to remember what it was her mother had done to make their father's blues disappear. Henry was just a second grader, and if even he could see that their father wasn't getting any better, it meant Serena was failing, and failing big-time. Every question he asked made her feel like a big, fat loser.

Keeping her back to her brother, Serena emptied the trash and hurried out of the kitchen to the garbage pail outside. After slamming the lid down, Serena stood next to the garbage can and took a deep breath. The night air was frigid, but it helped cool off the hot flash of anger she was feeling. Henry wasn't the one she should be mad at, she told herself.

She looked up into the pitch-black sky and sent up a prayer. What she would give for someone to come and help her. Somebody who wouldn't take them out of their home or put their father away. Someone who could solve their problems so all she would have to do was go to school and think about the play. That would be so wonderful.

Taking another deep breath, Serena walked slowly back to the house, trying to figure out how she could respond to her little brother's questions when she didn't know the answers herself.

Friday evening, while Serena was cleaning up
the kitchen after a dinner of chicken fingers and Tater
Tots, the phone rang. She hurried to answer it, hoping it
was Elijah. Instead, as soon as she said "Hello" she heard
"Superstar!" It was Uncle Peter.

"How's the play going, sweetie?"

Serena smiled. "Dang, Uncle Peter, it's about time you
called me back!" she answered. "The play is wonderful!
You're going to come see it, right? You won't forget, will
you?"

"I'll be at every one of your performances. I'll even put
all my honeys on hold for you, baby girl. I get to sit in the
VIP section, right?"

"Oh, ew, Uncle Peter, I don't want to hear about your
goofy girlfriends," Serena said with a groan. "I'll make sure
that you get a front-row seat, 'kay?"

"Thank you." Uncle Peter laughed. "And why are you
calling my girlfriends goofy?"

Serena laughed right back. "'Cause that last lady you brought to meet us was real goofy, and 'cause Mom always said you have rotten taste in women."

"Now see, you shouldn't be eavesdropping on grown folks' talk," Uncle Peter said, trying to sound stern. "And which one did I bring that was so goofy?"

"I wasn't eavesdropping. Mom told you right in front of me when you were leaving. She said, 'Don't you dare bring that goofy woman back to this house, Peter Charles Shaw.' Don't you remember? It was the woman who only ate yellow and green food, because that was the 'color of the earth at its healthiest.' She was pretty, though. Of course, they're always pretty."

"Oh yeah, Deborah. Yeah, all right, she was goofy. Okay, enough with talking to you, especially if you're going to dog out my ladies just like your wonderful momma used to, God bless her soul. Put your knucklehead dad on. That punk owes me about ten return phone calls."

"Yeah, sure. But Uncle Peter, can I, um, talk to you about a few things first?"

"Yeah, kid, just let me holler at your dad for a sec, and then we'll talk."

"Um, sure, hold on," she mumbled into the phone. Finally someone she could talk to about her father and she couldn't get him to listen. She sighed and jogged upstairs. She took a deep breath before knocking on the door.

"Dad?"

"Come in."

Serena opened the door to find her father sitting on the bed, surrounded by papers. She brightened a little. Finally, he wasn't sleeping!

"Dad, Uncle Peter is on the phone."

Her father sighed. "Tell him I'll call him back. I'm in the middle of something."

"Well, he said you owe him, like, a zillion return phone calls."

He ran a weary hand across his face. "Just tell him . . . never mind, I need to ask him if he wants my camera anyway."

"Your brand-new camera?" Serena asked. "Your Nikon D80? Why would you give him that? You've barely used it." She could still remember the look of joy on her father's face when her mother had given it to him for his birthday. "It was the last thing that Mom gave you."

He nodded, but it seemed that he hadn't heard a word she'd said.

She pointed to the phone on his nightstand. "Uncle Peter, remember?"

Her father nodded and reached for the phone. Putting his hand over the mouthpiece he said, "Hey, grab me a folder or extra-large envelope, please."

Serena left to grab an envelope from her father's office,

and when she returned, she heard her father telling Uncle Peter that he could also have his golf clubs.

"Yeah, I'm serious," he said. "I'm over it."

Well, that's just plain weird, Serena thought. Since taking up golf a few years before, her father had become totally obsessed with the game. He hadn't played lately, of course, because of his bluc, but Serena had never doubted he'd start it up again eventually. She gave her father a curious glance, tossing the envelope on the bed next to him. He riffled through the scattered papers on the bed, then shoved a stack of them into the envelope and handed it to her. Covering the mouthpiece again he said quietly, "Family papers. Can you put them somewhere safe?"

Okay, he's not better, Serena thought as she hurried out of the room. *He's gone completely crazy.*

WHEN THE PHONE RANG AGAIN, SERENA WAS SURE THAT IT must be Elijah. She picked up the phone and, in her sultriest tone, purred, "Good evening."

"Hey, I, um, Serena, is that you?" It was Uncle Peter again.

"Oh, hi."

"Sorry about that. Your dad basically hung up on me and I didn't get a chance to talk to you after. I know you wanted to tell me something."

143

"Well, yeah," Serena said flatly. "I did. It's just that . . . Dad's not doing well."

"Well, he did sound bummed when I talked to him, that's for sure. But of course, I expect him to be, for a good long while, with everything that's happened."

"Yeah, I know," Serena said. "But there's something else. He's . . ."

"It's all right, Serena, honey. You can tell me anything, you know that, right? I am your godfather, after all. That's what I'm here for. That, and easy money and expensive gifts. So what's going on?"

Serena swallowed the lump that had appeared in her throat, but when she finally spoke her voice was shaky. "Dad is . . . I don't know. I guess he's real blue."

Uncle Peter let out a little laugh. "How 'blue' exactly? Are we talking baby blue or like dark midnight?"

"Well, he's been in the same pajamas for about two weeks. I've kind of lost track. He never leaves the house. He doesn't really eat. He won't answer the phone. He isn't working. I can't remember the last time he did much of anything, except sleep. And cry. I mean, he was real sad and quiet right after Mom died, but then he kind of got better. But lately, it's like the blue came back and it's worse than it was before."

"Look, superstar," Uncle Peter said quietly. "I don't know if you knew this already, but your father suffers from depression. There's a history of it in our family. But your dad's always gotten through it just fine, with medication. Maybe he just needs to start taking a different dose. Why don't you see if you can get him to go to the doctor?"

"The doctor?" asked Serena. "How am I supposed to get him to the doctor?" Parents were the ones who were supposed to take their kids to the doctor, not the other way around.

"I'm sure you'll think of something, superstar," Uncle Peter said.

"Okay, I'll try," Serena said, but she was doubtful. She was pretty sure there was no way she'd be able to convince her father to go to the doctor. Getting him to go to the grocery store had been hard enough. Besides, why did she have to be responsible for everything? Serena frowned at the phone. This was a little help, but not as much as she needed, that was for darn sure.

"I would come down there right now and straighten him out myself," Uncle Peter told her, "but I'm sitting at the Heathrow airport in London waiting for a flight to Istanbul as we speak. I'm gone for about two weeks, but the minute I get back I'll try and make it there, how's that? I know you can handle things until then, sweetie. You got a lot of your momma in you. Hang in there, okay? I gotta run. They're almost done boarding. Love you, superstar."

* * *

AN HOUR LATER, ELIJAH DID CALL, BUT AFTER THE CON-versation with Uncle Peter, Serena wasn't in the mood to chitchat. Everything they talked about seemed silly and unimportant, and finally he told her she should go to bed. She sounded tired, he said. And major singing stars need their sleep. Gratefully, she hung up, hoping that her total lack of conversation hadn't completely turned him off.

Lying in bed, Serena found herself tossing and turning. No matter how she tried, she couldn't get Uncle Peter's words out of her head. Finally, she gave up trying to sleep and rolled out of bed. She walked down to the kitchen and turned on the family computer. Uncle Peter had said that her father suffered from depression, but what did that mean exactly? Frowning, Serena did an online search for the word "depression." Listed at the very top of the search results was a Web site about depression and its symptoms.

Suffering from five or more of these symptoms within the same two-week period may be a sign of major depression, particularly if these symptoms are not a by-product of another illness, drug abuse, or pre-scription medications.

Serena leaned forward and began to read the list of symptoms.

Symptom one: Depressed mood.

The first symptom of being depressed was being depressed? *Well, duh,* Serena thought. She rolled her eyes before continuing down the list.

Symptom two: Decreased interest or pleasure in daily activities.

Well, that fit. Showering was a daily activity and based on the funk in her father's room she bet he hadn't bathed in a few weeks.

Symptom three: Weight changes.

That fit, too! Her father was definitely getting skinny, and he almost never ate.

Symptom four: Sleep disturbances (either an inability to sleep or sleeping too much).

Serena's father *definitely* slept too much. So far he was four for four.

The next few symptoms were things Serena didn't understand. What on earth was "psychomotor agitation"? But when she came to "Symptom eight: Deep fatigue or loss of energy," Serena was certain that Uncle Peter was right—her father was obviously depressed. But if he refused to go to the doctor or take his medicine, what was she supposed to do about it?

Serena was about to close the browser when something on the screen caught her eye.

Signs of Suicide

She stared at the computer, her mind racing. Daddy wouldn't do that, would he? He was depressed, sure, but suicidal? No way. He wouldn't be thinking about *that*. Her father knew that he was all she and Henry had left. He wouldn't dare. Would he?

Gritting her teeth, Serena continued to read.

There are several signs that, if spotted early, can lead to prevention and treatment. These signs include, but are not limited to: depression, tension, nervousness, and anxiety.

"No," Serena said to the computer. "He's depressed, but he wouldn't . . ."

Those who suffer from depression are at a high risk of suicide. Of those who commit suicide, 90 percent have clinical depression.

Serena's eyes began to blur. She couldn't take it anymore. She didn't want to think about these sorts of things. Her eyes wet, she powered off the computer and scurried to her room before any tears could fall.

15

Early Saturday morning, as Serena lay in bed trying to banish another terrifying dream from her head, she found herself thinking about something the Scarecrow says in *The Wizard of Oz*, when the four main characters are creeping through the forest.

"I think it will get darker before it gets lighter."

She hoped that wasn't true.

Henry burst through her bedroom door.

"Sissy! Come see!" he shouted. He ran over and grabbed her hand, trying to pull her out of bed.

"Don't call me sissy," she snapped. "You know I hate that. Stop pulling on me." She was about to pull the covers over her head when a shock of fear ran through her. "What is it? Is it Dad?" She bolted out of bed.

"No, it's my pictures!" Henry said. "You gotta come see! They're the best ever!"

"Boy, you making a fuss about some picture you drew?"

Serena sank back into bed. "You've always got a drawing you want someone to see."

Henry pulled on her hand again.

"Yeah, but these ones are the bestest pictures I drew in my whole life!" he said. "I used Daddy's art stuff." Henry held up his hands right in front of her face, practically touching her nose. His fingertips were blue.

"Oooh, you're gonna get it," Serena said, pulling his hands farther from her face so she could see them better. If there was one ironclad rule in their house it was that no one, not even their mother, could touch their father's art supplies. Even using one of his pencils for homework was a surefire way to get grounded for a week. Not to mention a long, boring lecture about the expense of art supplies and their "absolute necessity for my line of work, which pays the bills around here."

"Nah-uh," Henry said, shaking his head furiously. "Daddy told me this morning I could have a whole bunch of his art stuff. His pencils, and his fancy crayons, and his don't-touch-it paper. Come see."

With a feeling of unexplained dread, Serena followed Henry into his mess of a room. Sure enough, on his desk were their father's art supplies. She picked up one of the giant drawing pads and read the faded price tag—$11.79.

Serena picked up a case of colored pencils and found

the price. $100.09. A set of "Soft Oil Pastels Made in Paris" in a beautiful wooden box cost $449.

"Whoa," Serena said quietly. Her father had just given a seven-year-old more than $600 worth of professional art supplies.

"I know!" Henry gushed. "And it's not even my birthday!" He gently took the wooden box out of Serena's hands and began rearranging his very expensive art supplies neatly on his desk.

"Look, siss—er, Serena. My first picture is of Daddy!" Henry held up a picture that explained his blue fingers. Using a variety of the blue pastels, he had created a single dark blue figure standing alone in a blue background. While the figure was one solid navy blue, the background was varying shades of blue. It was beautiful.

"Wow, Henry," said Serena, holding up the picture. "You're like some sort of freaky art prodigy."

"Hey!" Henry said angrily. "*You're* a freak. Get out! I'm not even going to show you the picture I did of you. You're mean!"

"No, please," Serena said. "I want to see it! I didn't mean to be mean. I was just trying to tell you how talented you are!"

Henry stuck his tongue out at her, but then opened one of the big tablets and held it out to her.

"It's not done yet," he said.

He'd drawn her in profile, completely black like a silhouette. He'd gotten the shape of her nose perfectly, and had added a pretty decent-looking ponytail, too, although she didn't think her forehead was nearly as big as he had drawn it. Behind her profile, Henry had begun to color the background with the same varying shades of blue he'd used for their father's picture. When he was finished, Serena would be silhouetted by the blue, just like in the lyrics from her favorite Broadway song.

"It's beautiful, Henry," Serena told him in awe. Somehow Henry had drawn exactly how she had been feeling for the last few weeks—like she was standing somewhere all alone, completely surrounded by her father's depression, encircled by his blue.

Henry tilted his head and stared down at his artwork in a serious, critical fashion. He looked up and nodded.

"Yep," he said firmly. "That's you."

Serena was in the middle of making grilled cheese sandwiches and tomato soup that afternoon when the doorbell rang.

Uncle Peter! she thought. He must have turned right around and flown here instead of Istanbul. Finally, someone capable of getting her father back to normal. She ran to the door and yanked it open. But standing on the porch, grinning at her, was Elijah.

"What are you doing here?" Serena asked.

"Well, hello, to you, too," Elijah said. "I'll have you know that I was invited over."

"Uh, I don't remember inviting you," Serena said. She put a hand on her hip, pretending that she was in her cutest outfit and not her faded, too-short, pink cotton candy pajamas.

"I invited him over."

She turned and saw Henry behind her. *"Hola, Elijah!"* he said, squeezing around Serena and extending his hand to Elijah. They performed some silly, overly complicated handshake. "Serena, move, so Elijah can come in."

Reluctantly, Serena stepped to the side and let Elijah in. When she turned around, she suddenly noticed the state of their house. A teetering stack of unread newspapers lay by the front door. Piles of mail were tossed onto the foyer table and scattered on the floor beneath. Henry's coats, sweaters, and baseball hats trailed up the staircase, along with a good number of his toys and drawings from school. Serena stared at the mess in dismay. Why hadn't she noticed it before? Probably the only clean places in the house were the dining room and the kitchen.

The kitchen!

"Oh, crap! Our lunch is burning!" Serena shouted. She rushed into the kitchen and flipped over the slightly blackened sandwich and turned the heat down on the now-boiling tomato soup.

"So what gourmet meal have you prepared this afternoon?" Elijah asked as he strolled into the kitchen.

"It eez a culinary masterpiece," Serena said in a fake French accent. "Zee grilled cheese and zee tomato zoup."

"I see that your French is just about as good as your Spanish," Elijah said with a laugh. "Whoa, you like your grilled cheese well-done, eh?" He had walked over to Serena and was peering over her shoulder, standing so close that she thought she could actually feel the heat of his body through her pj's.

"Oh, well, it was browning perfectly," Serena said, trying to keep her voice steady. "And then someone rudely interrupted my cooking."

"Oh, snap, my bad," Elijah said with a chuckle.

Serena scooped up the sandwich with the spatula and held it aloft, but then realized that to get the plate she needed, she would have to turn her body away completely from Elijah, and at the moment she wasn't very interested in doing that.

"Oh, sorry," Elijah said softly in her ear. *"Te adoro."*

Serena growled deeply in her throat. Elijah laughed, but moved a few steps back.

"You guys are weird," Henry announced. He had been sitting so quietly at the kitchen table that Serena had forgotten all about him.

"What?" Elijah and Serena said in unison.

155

Henry rolled his eyes and then began to make kissy noises.

Elijah started laughing, and Serena slid the sandwich onto a plate, and then threw the spatula at Henry, who ducked just in time.

Serena didn't think she could possibly feel any more mortified, but then, out of nowhere, her father appeared.

Dressed in his usual soiled pajamas, he stood at the kitchen door, and the smell of his unwashed body quickly permeated the room. Serena's heart started beating so fast she was sure that she would be the first person in history to actually die of embarrassment, which was absolutely fine with her as long as it happened quickly.

Elijah stepped forward, his hand outstretched. For some reason, he looked thrilled to see Serena's father.

"Hello, sir," he said, his voice an octave higher than usual. "I'm Elijah Mills. I'm a friend of Serena's from school. I'm the set designer for the play. Henry's helping me with the sets and he wanted me to come over and see some poppies."

"Poppies?" her father asked. Serena couldn't help thinking that any *normal* father would have had the decency to be outraged, or at the very least curious, as to why some strange boy was standing in his kitchen with his daughter, who was still dressed in her pajamas. But *her* crazy, depressed, overly blue father simply looked at Elijah with barely a spark of interest in his eyes, and ignored Elijah's hand.

"Yeah," Elijah said. "It's a real short scene, but that doesn't mean it shouldn't look as nice as possible. I mean, it's one of the times in the play that the sets are integral to the story, you know, not just pretty scenery, but almost like a character."

"Scenery," her father muttered.

Serena glanced at his face and realized that he had no idea what Elijah was talking about. She wished she had her spatula back so she could throw it at her *father's* head.

"The play, Daddy," Serena said through clenched teeth. "You know, *The Wiz*. I'm Dorothy. The lead role."

Her father stood for a moment staring at her.

"Oh," he mumbled. "Yeah. That's right."

"I think you'll be impressed with the sets," Elijah told him, apparently not noticing how oddly he was behaving. "Little man, I mean, Henry, has your artistic talent, which you probably already know. I'd love for you to come by and give us your opinion. I've always loved your illustrations. I still have my original copy of *If I Were in Charge*! I look at it for inspiration sometimes. Your artwork is, well, it's off the hook!"

"Oh," her father repeated. He didn't seem to be listening to Elijah anymore. Serena could see him mentally retreating from the kitchen, from the conversation, even as he stood right there next to her not physically moving an inch.

"Maybe you can come to rehearsal one day next week and take a look at everything," Elijah went on, his face lit with excitement. "See what touches you'd recommend!"

Serena was looking right at Henry then, so she saw his face fall when her father replied, "I don't think so."

"Oh, yeah," Elijah said casually, but Serena heard the disappointment in his voice. "I'm sure you're very busy. I know you're working on the next book in the Priscilla series."

"That's right," her father muttered, more to himself than to Elijah—as if his work was something he hadn't thought about in a while. "Excuse me." Then he headed downstairs without a backward glance at any of them.

Elijah turned to Serena and Henry as if hoping for an explanation for their father's odd behavior. Before Serena could think of a response, Henry said, "Daddy's got the blue."

Elijah's eyebrows shot up.

"Excuse me, I gotta get dressed," Serena mumbled, before dashing out of the room. She hoped Elijah hadn't noticed the tears in her eyes.

Serena stood under the shower letting the water mix with her tears before washing them away. She was torn between hurrying out so she could hang with Elijah

158

and Henry, and staying in there until she was sure that Elijah had left. But when the hot water began to run out, she exited and got dressed. She headed back to the kitchen, but found it empty and, surprisingly, clean. All the dirty dishes were in the dishwasher, and the skillet and pot had been washed and were sitting on the counter, drying. She was thrilled for a second—until it dawned on her in a burst of embarrassment that Elijah must have convinced Henry to help him tidy up.

She sat down at the kitchen table and put her head in her hands. She was exhausted. All the sleepless nights were getting to her. She had just closed her eyes for a little catnap when she heard footsteps behind her. Her father was walking up from the basement, carrying a framed picture. He headed out of the kitchen and up the stairs without a word, as if he hadn't even noticed Serena. She stood and followed him.

Serena's father knocked on Henry's door. Peering over her father's shoulder, Serena could see that Elijah and Henry were hard at work on the poppies that Henry had been drawing that morning.

"Young man?" her father said. He held the picture out, gesturing for Elijah to come and take it from him. "Thank you for your kind words about my work. Here, I thought you might like to have this."

Serena stood on her tiptoes so she could see what her father had given Elijah.

"Oh, you have got to be shi—er, kidding me!" Elijah exclaimed. "I can't take this! This is, like, the original, isn't it?"

Serena's father shrugged. "I'd be happy for you to have it." He laughed grimly. "It might even be worth something someday."

Serena stepped around her father and stood next to Elijah, who was holding up the picture, admiring it with a sort of happy, dazed look on his face. In his arms he held the framed original artwork of the cover of *If I Were in Charge*, her father's first book. For as long as Serena could remember, that painting had hung directly over her father's desk in his office.

"Sir, I can't take this," Elijah said. His proper manners made Serena feel all melty inside. Who knew someone who could be such a smart-ass could also be a gentleman?

"Please take it. It should belong to someone who will enjoy it and appreciate it." Her father looked at the picture with affection. "Please."

"This is off the chain!" Elijah shouted, all of his composure gone. "You even signed it!"

Even though her father sounded calm and rational, something about the way he was behaving didn't set right with Serena. Why was he suddenly giving away all his things? What was going on in his head? It made her nervous.

"Thank you, Mr. Shaw, this is an awesome honor,"

Elijah gushed. "This is the best gift I've ever been given. Ever. Thank you."

Serena's father nodded, then turned and walked away. Serena followed him down the hall and, trotting to catch up with him, grabbed his arm.

"Daddy, what are you doing?" she asked him.

Her father looked down at her, gently touched her cheek, and gave her arm a gentle squeeze before turning and walking away.

16

Nothing in the last four chapters of *The Outsiders* could hold Serena's attention that night. Her mind kept wandering back to Elijah, how he'd pulled her away from Henry and asked her to a movie later that evening. She'd almost said yes. Almost.

"I wish I could, but I got Henry duty tonight," she'd told him, a lump forming in her throat. If she went out with Elijah, who would keep an eye on Henry and make sure he ate dinner and didn't burn down the house or do anything else stupid? Not to mention the fact that she hadn't done laundry in more than a week, which meant she and Henry would be running low on underwear soon. And the house was a mess, too. Now that she'd noticed it she couldn't take living in the filth another minute. "Can I get a rain check? Please?"

Elijah had nodded, looking sympathetic—the last embarrassing nail in a coffin full of humiliating stuff.

Serena tossed her English book aside with a burst of

anger as she remembered all the cleaning she'd done after Elijah left. Her father had been home all day long! Doing nothing! The least he could do was pick up after himself. What kind of parent was he? Totally useless.

But then her mind wandered to the scene in Henry's room. She couldn't remember the last time her father had actually talked so much. Maybe he was getting better. God, wouldn't *that* be great? If he got out of his blue, Serena wouldn't have to do the laundry for everyone anymore. It would mean no more grocery shopping or cooking. Serena would finally be able to focus on stuff *she* wanted to. She could hang out with Kat and Nikka again on weekends. They could triple date! Kat and Ian, Nikka and Marcus, and she and Elijah. Movies on Saturday nights, or maybe bowling. That would be so awesome—just being a normal kid.

Smiling to herself, Serena pulled the pillow off her face and tucked it under her head. For a minute, she allowed herself to believe that she really could be normal again. And she fell asleep happy, dreaming of dating Elijah.

SERENA WAS LAUGHING, SURROUNDED BY ENDLESS FIELDS *of paper flowers. She and Elijah were having a picnic. Elijah leaned in closer to her and whispered something in Spanish. Serena swatted him playfully. He caught her hand and pulled her in closer. Serena tilted her head and closed her eyes. All of*

the sudden she heard an alarm. No, no, she whispered to Elijah.
It's okay, you can kiss me.

Serena woke up to the sound of the smoke alarm blaring, again. She stomped out of her room toward the kitchen.

"Yo! Pinhead!" she yelled at Henry. He was standing on top of the kitchen table, frantically fanning the smoke away from the alarm with an oven mitt. "You woke me up!" Serena opened the back door and turned on the ceiling fan. Then she snatched the toaster's plug out of the outlet and began fishing the stuck and blackened bagel out with a butter knife. "Get down off the table, stupid," she said once the smoke alarm had stopped.

"Don't call me stupid," Henry snapped, scrambling off the table.

"Yeah, well, any dimwit who can't fix a bagel is just about as stupid as stupid can get."

"What's your problem?" Henry said, grabbing another bagel out of the bag and hacking at it with a knife.

"I was sleeping," Serena answered. She snatched the bagel and knife out of his hand. She knew she was being mean, but she couldn't seem to stop herself. "You're going to cut a finger off, genius. Give that here."

"I was sleeping, I was sleeping," Henry mimicked. "So what? I was hungry."

Serena tried to take a few deep breaths to calm down, but she was just so annoyed. The smoke alarm ruining one of the few good dreams she'd had in ages was just the last straw. She shoved the bagel into the slots and pushed the toaster button down, but it popped up immediately. "If you're so hungry, try something simple next time. Like cereal. You shouldn't be able to screw that up too much." She shoved the button down again.

"There's no more milk left, *genius*," Henry answered.

"Oh, great," Serena said, pushing the toaster's lever again and again. "We're out of milk *and* you've broken the toaster."

Henry rolled his eyes at her. "Try plugging it back in, stupid."

"You're a pain in my butt," Serena said. She shoved the cord back into the outlet. "I'm tired of cleaning up after you, and having to watch you after school, and cooking for you, and doing everything around the house. You can't do *anything*!" Serena continued, her voice trembling with anger. "You are totally useless. You're just a bunch of extra work for me! And stop leaving your crap all over the house! I'm not your friggin' maid!"

With that, Serena turned and stormed out of the kitchen. She headed back to her room, slammed her bedroom door, and crawled back into bed. But after tossing and turning for several minutes, she knew it was useless. She'd never get back to sleep and finish her dream, because every time she closed her eyes the image that kept popping into her head was of Henry's face as he stood there and listened to her scream at him. The last of her anger dribbled away, leaving her feeling nothing but guilt.

"Crap," she muttered. "Crap, crap, crap."

Serena flipped the covers off her head and took a deep breath—just like she did before she belted out a long note in rehearsal. She had to pull herself together. If she lost it, then Henry would be all alone.

Serena rolled out of bed and headed back to the kitchen to apologize to Henry. But just as she stepped into the room the phone started ringing.

"Hello?"

"Superstar! How's it going?" It was Uncle Peter, and the connection was awful.

"Not good, Uncle Peter," Serena said, plopping down at the table next to Henry. He had turned his back to her the minute she entered the kitchen. "I think I'm losing it. I just yelled at Henry for nothing and I feel real bad about it. I'm really sorry, 'cause he's a cool kid and he doesn't deserve me bugging out on him like that." Henry continued to eat his dry cereal with his back to her, but she knew he was listening. "I hope he'll forgive me. He's the best little brother there is, and I'd hate for him to stay mad at me. When can you get home? I need help!"

She waited a moment for a response, but there was only silence on the other end of the phone.

"Hello? Uncle Peter? You still there?"

More silence.

"Aw, man, we must have gotten disconnected," Serena muttered. She tried calling Uncle Peter's cell a few times but it went straight to voice mail. "I bet he forgot to charge his cell again. He's a goofball."

She turned and looked at her brother. "Look, Henry," she said, scooting her chair closer to him. "I'm totally sorry that I yelled at you and said all those awful things. I didn't mean them. Well, except for the cleaning up after yourself part. That I *did* mean. It's just that, with Dad being so blue, I've had to do a bunch of extra stuff and sometimes I feel . . . it's just too much . . ." Serena's voice trailed away. "How about I make you some waffles? Wouldn't that taste way better than that dry old cereal? Do you forgive me for being a stupid jerk?"

Henry looked up at her. His eyes were dry, but she could see the white streaks of dried tears on his cheeks. Suddenly he flung his arms around her and gave her a tight, long hug. Serena sat there next to her little brother for a good long while, letting him hold her. And holding him back.

LATE SUNDAY EVENING, SERENA HEADED SLOWLY DOWN the hallway to her father's door. She had to get him to go to the doctor, she knew that now. He needed more help than she could give him.

Serena took a deep breath before knocking quietly.

There was no response. She knocked a little more forcefully. Still nothing. Swallowing back the panic that had risen to her throat, Serena opened the door.

An old VCR tape of her parents' wedding was playing on her father's TV, and the flickering images were the only source of light in the room. Serena stared at the screen for a moment, entranced by the sight of her parents in their youth. They looked so happy, totally oblivious to everyone around them.

A soft snort caught Serena's attention. Turning reluctantly away from the screen, she saw the lump of rumpled bed linen that was her father. She sighed. Maybe if she let him sleep, if he got a good night's rest, he'd be better in the morning. She could convince him to go to the doctor then.

No, she thought. *No*. She needed to talk to her father now.

Serena had never considered herself a chicken. After all, she had no problem strolling onto a stage and singing a song in front of a bunch of people, even her classmates, who could be real idiots. But for some reason, she didn't have the guts to even think about what might be wrong with her father—or worse, what might happen if she couldn't get him the help he needed. Clearly she was more Cowardly Lion than Dorothy at the moment. *Brave*, she thought. *I need to think about being brave.*

Serena closed her eyes and pictured how she would look

in the spotlight with her costume on. Her mind wandered to one of her favorite songs in the play, where Dorothy sang to the Lion about courage.

"You're standing strong and tall."

She sang the tune quietly at first, trying out the phrasing that Mr. Hobbs had suggested, which she wasn't all that crazy about.

"You're the bravest of them all!"

She sang a little louder, trying a half step down at the end note. That was more like it. Squeezing her eyes shut tight, she belted out the last phrase of the song:

"You're a lion,
in your own way.
Be a lion!"

A burst of applause caught her attention. Turning back to the television screen, Serena saw her mother and father give each other a long, lingering, movie-like kiss and climb into a white stretch limousine. They were laughing and waving and holding each other's hands, looking as though they would never have a sad day in their lives.

Serena shook her father. "Dad?" Serena said as soon as he blinked his eyes open. He didn't respond. "Dad! Wake up. You need to see a doctor."

"Huh?"

"A doctor," Serena repeated. "I'm going to make you an appointment with Dr. Zarlengo." She held up her father's leather address book, which she'd found in the kitchen. "I'll call for you if you want. First thing in the morning. Maybe you can even get in tomorrow."

Her father turned and looked at her without saying anything.

"Nah, I'm good," he answered at last. "I just gotta think some things over."

"Dad, you need to go." Serena pictured herself onstage again, pumping herself full of courage. "There's something wrong. You're freaking me out and you're scaring Henry. You need to go to a doctor and get help."

There. She'd said it. He'd have to listen to that, wouldn't he?

Her father sighed. "A doctor," he said softly. "Sure, baby. I guess."

Serena brightened. "So that's a yes? You'll call tomorrow?" She could hardly believe it.

Her father nodded his head, then with a final shrug of his shoulders he buried himself under his covers again, quickly falling back to sleep.

Serena stood, watching him, until on the television her parents' wedding video faded to black, finally flicking to the hideous bright blue that marked the end of the tape.

Serena sighed and left the room, shutting the door behind her. She was beginning to hate the color blue.

17

When Serena finally got in touch with Uncle
Peter, he wasn't as helpful as she had hoped he
would be. She wanted him to say that he'd fly out to help
them that minute, that he'd force her father to go to his
doctor's appointment tomorrow. But what he said instead
was, "It's past seven here. I've got to get up and go to a
meeting this morning, but then I'll rearrange the rest of
my schedule so I can get out of here as soon as humanly
possible. With any luck I can be back in the country by
Wednesday. Sound good, superstar?"

Three whole days. Serena didn't think she could last
three more minutes. But she swallowed a sob and nodded
anyway—until she remembered that her uncle couldn't
see her over the phone. "Okay. I'm sorry to be a bother,
Uncle Peter."

"Are you kidding? You're my favorite niece. It's the
least I can do."

Serena laughed softly, despite her fear and sadness. "I'd be real flattered to hear that, except I'm your only niece."

"Well, I didn't say there was a lot of competition for that coveted spot, but nevertheless you're among the top ten on my favorite people list."

"Top ten? I thought I'd be number one."

"Hey, don't get too pushy, or you'll drop right off the list."

"Thank you, Uncle Peter," Serena said, smiling into the phone. "You are my absolute favorite uncle."

"Hey, I'm your only uncle."

Serena laughed. "I didn't say there was a lot of competition."

"Hey, that's my joke, you little comedy thief," Uncle Peter said with a chuckle. "Get some sleep, superstar. I'll be there as soon as possible. We'll get your dad all squared away, and then in March the three devastatingly handsome and charming Shaw men will all sit front row for opening night and cheer for you like we're at a football game. Then I'll take you to the best restaurant in town to celebrate. You still love Burger King, right?"

"Ha! You wish! I'm the star of the play. You better take me to the Dove. I plan to order lobster! And steak, too!"

"Whoa, I'd better start saving my money. Hang in there, Serena. Go to bed. And, Serena? I'm sure your father won't do anything crazy. I know you said there

173

were a lot of signs, but I bet it's just your imagination. Remember when you were little and you watched *Willy Wonka* one too many times, and you were sure that Oompa Loompas lived in the garden? You just need some sleep. I'll be there soon."

Get some sleep? *Not likely*, Serena thought. As much as she tried to convince herself that Uncle Peter was right, she knew one thing was true—this was very different from *Willy Wonka*.

Sure enough, her dreams were so bad that night that Serena didn't get more than four hours of sleep. When the alarm sounded Monday morning, she didn't know how she was going to drag herself out of bed, much less find the energy to get Henry to school and stay awake all day long. She wanted to call in sick so she could stay home and keep an eye on her father, make sure he made a doctor's appointment. But midterms were coming up, and she didn't think she had the leeway grade-wise to skip any classes. Anyway, Uncle Peter had told her not to worry. She didn't know about that, but as for leaving her father alone, well, she was going to have to step out on faith.

AFTER GETTING DRESSED AND REMINDING HER FATHER TO call for an appointment, Serena headed back to the kitchen, put a bagel in the toaster for Henry, and went upstairs to wake him up.

Peeking her head into Henry's room, she sang a perky

song about the morning from a movie she'd watched recently.

Henry rolled over, rubbed his eyes, and looked at her. "Huh?"

Serena sang her response, *"Yesterday my heart* something, something, something, I don't really know the words!"

"You're a weirdo," Henry declared, but he got up and staggered sleepily toward his dresser and pulled out some clean underwear. "What old dumb song are you singing now?"

"I don't know. Some song from an old movie, *The Band Wagon.* I watched it on Saturday. It was pretty good. Come on, hurry up, we gotta go in, like, fifteen minutes."

"But I'm hungry," whined Henry.

"I made you a bagel. Get a move on it."

"Okay, but be sure to put honey and whipped cream on it."

"You mean cream cheese."

"Yeah, duh, that's what I said. I want honey and cream cheese."

Serena gave him a salute and headed back to the kitchen. Her father was on the phone. When he saw her he lowered his voice. She pretended to ignore him, but listened to as much of his conversation as she could.

". . . yes, yes. I'll be there. Eleven o'clock. Thank you."

He was talking to the doctor's office! He was actually

making an appointment. She smiled at the bagel in her hand, and added this new seed of hope next to the one her uncle had planted in her mind, watering them both with a fervent prayer that either, or both, would grow.

Tuesday morning in math class, Serena couldn't get her mind to stay focused. Even though she'd slept better last night—knowing that her dad had finally gone to the doctor and had gotten medication, and that her uncle would be there tomorrow—it felt like there was still too much going on in her head for her to concentrate on anything.

"Please pass your homework to the front." Her math teacher's voice somehow penetrated through Serena's jumbled thoughts.

For a minute Serena couldn't remember if she had done her math homework. She riffled through her notebooks like everyone else, all the while retracing the events from yesterday afternoon. Rehearsal, walking home, cooking dinner, making her father take his new pills, homework . . . Homework! She *had* done her math. That and her Spanish had been all she could find the energy to do while she was waiting for the hot dogs to cook. She had tried to read for English and social studies, too, but she hadn't been able to keep her eyes open. That's when she'd given up and told Henry to go to sleep, and collapsed on her bed in her clothes.

Even later that afternoon, standing in the lunch line,

Serena wasn't paying attention to her surroundings. Instead she was trying to calculate how many more hours she had until Uncle Peter's arrival. It wasn't until a hand waved in front of her face that she realized someone was standing next to her.

"Hello, earth to Serena!" said Kat, adding a carton of chocolate milk to Serena's tray. "Hey, can you hook me up? I totally spent all my money last night at the café with Ian. Thanks!"

"Um, thanks for calling me back two weekends ago," Serena snapped. Actually she had forgotten all about Kat's not calling until that moment. But she still felt like she had a right to be angry about it. Nikka and Kat had been too busy with their own lives lately to pay attention to the mess that was hers. Some friends they were being.

"Oh, yeah, sorry," Kat said airily. "My bad. It's just that Ian and I were watching a movie together, well, together on the phone, you know." She sighed and Serena frowned at her.

"Whatever." Serena paid for her lunch—and Kat's milk—and wandered out of the line to survey the cafeteria. Kat didn't leave her side.

"So where's Nikka?" Serena asked when Kat started following her over to the table where Elijah was sitting.

"She's suspended."

"What? Get out!"

"Yeah, she has too many unexcused absences."

"Wait, that doesn't make sense," Serena said, settling down beside Elijah. Kat scooted in next to her, making her move closer—very close—to Elijah.

He leaned over and whispered in her ear, "*Cuando estoy tan cerca de ti, solo quiero besarte.*"

Serena growled at him before turning her attention back to Kat. "You know that makes no kind of sense, right?" she repeated. "Nikka's being punished for not coming to school by being told not to come to school?"

"Yeah, girl! I know, right?" Kat laughed before taking a big swig of chocolate milk. "Whatever. All I know is that she must have been missing more than just lunch period with me, 'cause girlfriend had, like, fifteen missed classes this past six weeks. She's totally out of pocket. Anyways." She took another gulp of milk. "My mom said she saw your dad at the clinic yesterday. He okay?"

"Well, I guess—I mean—" Serena stammered. The sudden change of subject caught her totally off guard. "He's been a little sick."

Kat helped herself to one of Serena's chicken nuggets. "Well, my mom was pretty worried about him. She said he came to the office in his pajamas. She said to ask you if he was okay."

Serena felt all the blood in her body rush to her face. She quickly stuffed a nugget in her mouth. She chewed slowly. "He's fine," she said at last. "Just under the weather."

"Mr. Shaw is by far the coolest adult I've ever met,"

Elijah said, leaning over to talk to Kat. "He gave me some one-of-a-kind, signed artwork. As far as I'm concerned he totally rocks."

"When have *you* met Mr. Shaw?" Kat asked. She looked from Elijah back to Serena, who shoved another piece of chicken into her mouth.

"On Saturday," Elijah answered casually. "When I was over at Serena's."

Serena was staring down at her food, but out of the corner of her eye she could still see Kat's eyes bug out and her mouth drop open. *Great,* Serena thought. Kat's mouth ran nonstop. Before school was over everyone in the seventh grade would think that she and Elijah were going out. But then, she thought to herself, maybe that wasn't such a bad thing, people thinking they were a couple . . .

"And why were you hanging at Serena's?" Kat asked Elijah, nudging Serena in the side.

"I was helping Henry do stuff for the play," he answered. Then he added, *"Y conocer a la familia de mi futura mujer."*

"Say what?" Kat said. "Dang, boy!" She turned to Serena. "How come you don't speak Spanish like that? Aren't y'all in the same Spanish class?"

"He's a big ole cheater, that's why," Serena said, happy to have the subject veer away from Elijah's visit to her house—and her father. "He already *knew* how to speak practically perfect Spanish before even taking that class." Elijah chuckled.

"Oh, snap! Talk about an easy A." Kat hooted and reached a fist out to get a little dap from Elijah. Before he could return the fist bump, Serena slapped both of their hands away.

"Girl, don't be giving him no props!" she scolded. "You know that's wrong. He makes everyone in the class look like we ain't studying hard enough. The teacher's all like, *'Elijah tiene los mejores gradas otra vez. El es nuestro mejor elefante.'* Every day. "

Elijah burst out laughing. "I have the best step and I'm the best elephant in class, huh, Serena Star? Man, you really suck at Spanish!"

Kat laughed along with Elijah. "Hey, Serena, don't hate the playa, girlfriend!"

Elijah grinned and added, *"Odio el juego, mi amor."*

Kat burst out laughing—and she didn't even take Spanish. She reached over and, using one hand to pin down Serena's arms, extended her other arm to Elijah again, who gave her a fist bump.

"Yeah, whatever," Serena said, trying not to laugh. She turned to Elijah. "Oh, and by the way, I understood what you just said. *Every* single word of it."

Elijah had no shame in his game. He simply smiled at her and winked. Before Serena could say anything else the bell rang, and they all hurried to clear their trays and head to their next class. And Serena couldn't help grinning the whole way.

18

It was past seven by the time Serena and Henry made it home. Even though she was bone tired, she was still floating on the high of the rehearsal. At least until she stepped into the house. Crossing the threshold was like walking into a graveyard.

Dinner was quiet. Serena sat picking at the frozen dinner she'd nuked for them, while Henry seemed to push most of his food from one side of his plate to the other, barely eating. An hour later, after sending a silent thanks to her teachers for a light night of homework, Serena put Henry to bed. All she wanted to do next was go to bed herself, but she felt compelled to search the house for her father. Since they'd been home, they hadn't seen or heard him. She'd put off looking for him as long as she could, scared of what she'd find.

First she checked his room. It was dark and empty. He wasn't upstairs at all, or on the first floor. The only place left was the basement. Serena trekked down the steps.

A beam of light shone through the crack under the office door. Serena opened it without knocking and was stunned to see her father sitting at his desk. He was drawing!

She took a curious step toward his desk.

"Yes?" he said, without raising his head.

"I didn't mean to disturb you, Daddy. I, um . . . I was just going to turn off the light. I didn't know you were in here."

Serena still couldn't believe what she was seeing—her father, hard at work again! The pills must really be working. Maybe this meant everything would be back to normal soon.

Her father finished the figure he was drawing and looked up at her.

For a minute he sat there staring at her as if he hadn't seen her in a long time.

"You'll grow to be a beautiful, vibrant woman," he said. "Just like your mother was." A look so sad crossed his face that Serena felt tears coming into her eyes.

"Thank you, Daddy," she said softly. She opened her mouth to tell him about Uncle Peter's visit tomorrow, but something made her snap her mouth closed. Maybe it would be best not to tell him. She stood watching him work on a new sketch for a few minutes, racking her brain for something else to say. Finally she pointed to the drawing on his desk. "What are you working on?" she asked him.

"Just my legacy," he said. Then he smiled one of the unhappiest smiles she'd ever seen.

Serena was so tired on Wednesday morning that she was halfway through first period before she remembered. Wednesday! Uncle Peter! Just the thought of walking into the house to find him there lifted her spirits. Suddenly she felt more awake. She straightened up in her seat and managed to pay attention the rest of class. During second period she actually caught herself humming. She couldn't remember the last time she had even *felt* like humming.

At lunch she went into the office to use the phone. She probably needed to tell her father about Uncle Peter's visit. Wouldn't he be so surprised when he saw him there?

Unfortunately, she found herself waiting for Myron to finish whining to his mother. Apparently his lunch was wrong again.

"I *know* I said the black olive hummus, Mom. You just didn't listen to me like always. Ranch dressing? Really, Mom, you *know* I don't do dairy," Myron griped. "No, a *vegan*, Mom. *Ve-gan*."

Serena caught one of the office ladies' eyes and made a face. The office lady snorted back a guffaw of laughter, then tried to pull a stern, quelling look back onto her face.

"Fine then, never mind. I will just be forced to eat the carrot sticks without a dip. Goodbye, Mother." Myron

183

hung up the phone. Turning, he saw Serena. "Moms! Who needs them?"

Serena took a step back as if he had punched her. Myron seemed to suddenly realize who he was talking to, and his hand flew to his mouth. "Er, sorry, Serena. My bad." He scurried out of the office.

Serena stood for a moment, fists clenched, trying to swallow down the lump in her throat. The office lady who had overheard looked at her sympathetically.

Only concentrating on how much she couldn't stand Myron Thomas allowed her to regain her composure. When she thought she could talk without her voice shaking, Serena dialed her home number. The phone rang and rang. She tried three times, but her father never answered. Then she tried calling her uncle Peter's number. It went directly to voice mail. Serena sighed. She was about to head to lunch when, for no reason at all, she dialed her mother's cell phone number. When it went to voice mail, Serena heard the voice she'd been missing for over a year.

"Hello, you've reached Vivian Shaw, vice president of Mergers and Expansion, Flat Iron Foods. Unfortunately, I'm unable to come to the phone at this time. Please leave a message after the beep, and I will get back to you as soon as possible."

Her father hadn't turned off her mother's phone. Serena was willing to bet years of allowance that he'd probably

184

been paying the bill for months, just to call and listen to that voice. Tears burned Serena's eyes. Glancing over at the office ladies and finding them preoccupied, she waited for the beep.

"I love you, Mommy," she whispered into the phone. "I miss you so much."

THAT NIGHT AFTER REHEARSAL, SHE MADE HENRY PRACTI-cally run home. She'd resisted telling him why she was in such a hurry, wanting to surprise him, but that just meant he acted like a baby all the way home.

"Sissy! Slow down," he whined. She slowed her pace for a moment, but a few minutes later she was running down the sidewalk again. She was so excited and relieved that Uncle Peter would finally be there, she couldn't help but feel like singing. One of her mother's favorite show tunes popped into her head, and Serena hummed happily as she hurried toward home. It seemed to take longer than normal to get to their house. If it hadn't been for Henry and his stumpy legs Serena would have run all the way.

When they got to their block Serena looked around for her uncle's car, but it was nowhere to be found. She looked up and down the street. Maybe he'd gotten a new car. He changed cars almost as often as he changed girlfriends—at least, that's what their mom used to say. But her heart sank when she realized that if he *had* gotten a new car, the house wouldn't be as dark as it was now, with no lights shining through the windows, just the way it usually was when they got home from school. Opening the door, Serena found the house quiet and tomb-like. The disappointment she felt was so strong it made her nauseous. Serena dropped her things and ran to the bathroom. She leaned over the toilet, but nothing came up. Eventually the nausea faded and was replaced by sobs of frustration.

Serena sat on the toilet and cried until Henry knocked on the door. She turned on the water and splashed her face, and was about to use a hand towel to dry herself when she noticed how filthy it was. Henry had used it to clean up his paint.

Serena yanked the door open and threw the towel in Henry's face.

"Hey, idiot, you ruined the towel!" she screamed.

Henry took a step back from her, his eyes wide. He looked from her face to the towel at his feet.

"But you said to clean up the paint," he said.

"With a rag, you moron. Jeez!"

Henry burst into tears and ran up to his room, which only made Serena more angry.

She was just about to yell at him again when the phone rang. She snatched it and answered.

"Yeah," she growled.

"Serena? Is that you? This is your uncle Peter."

"Where the hell are you?" Serena screamed into the

phone. "You said you'd be here and you're not! You lied to me!"

"Whoa," her uncle Peter said. "Calm down. Look, I . . ."

"I don't need excuses, I need help!" Serena's voice cracked. "You said you'd be here!"

"Serena," her uncle said sternly. "You need to watch your tone. You know better than to talk to an adult in that way."

Serena burst into tears. Long, loud, ragged, gut-wrenching sobs. Her uncle *never* reprimanded her. Ever. He sounded just like her father would have if he were his normal self again.

"Whoa, breathe, sweetie," her uncle said softly. "Look, I missed the early flight out of Istanbul yesterday, and now I'm stuck in London. The airport's fogged in. All flights out tonight are canceled, and they're expecting a blizzard tomorrow. But I swear to you I'm on my way. I will be there by Friday. No later. I promise, even if I have to rent a rowboat and paddle there myself."

Serena took a few shuddering breaths, trying to calm down.

"Superstar, you hang in there. I'm on my way. Everything will be okay. Why don't you put my pinhead brother on the phone, okay?"

Serena heaved a sigh, set the phone down on the counter, and went to look for her father, swiping her face and grabbing a tissue for her nose.

It took her a few minutes to find him. He was in *her* room, standing at her desk with an envelope in his hand.

"Oh, hey, Daddy," she said. "Um, Uncle . . ."

"Why are these papers I gave you here?"

Serena was surprised by the tone of his voice. It was one that she hadn't heard from him in God knows how long. It threw her off for a moment.

"Um, huh?"

"These papers," he said, waving them at her. "These *very important* papers I gave you. They were buried under this pile of stuff on your desk."

"I, well . . ." Serena said.

"Didn't I tell you to keep track of them?"

Serena honestly couldn't remember what he had said. She shrugged her shoulders in answer.

Her father glared at her for a moment before heading out of her room. "I'm going to put them in the top drawer of my desk in the office. Do you understand me?"

"Yeah, Dad," Serena said warily.

"Are you sure?" her father snapped, stopping at her door. "Where am I going to put these very important papers?"

"In the top drawer of your desk in your office."

"Fine. Remember that."

He stormed out of her room then, leaving Serena staring after him, totally confused. It was a minute before she remembered why she'd been looking for him in the first place.

"Dad!" she called, running after him. He was already down in his office by the time she reached him. "Uncle Peter's on the phone. He wants to talk to you."

Her father rubbed his face, and Serena suddenly noticed that he almost had a beard now. All anger in his eyes had disappeared.

"Oh."

He closed his desk drawer, then turned and walked out of the office.

"Are you going to get the phone?" she asked, her head dizzy from all his mood swings.

He sighed one of his sad, pitiful sighs. "Yeah, I guess." He headed up the stairs to his room.

Serena hurried back to the kitchen and picked up the extension to let her uncle know that her father was coming. But before she could say anything, her father picked up. Serena pressed her ear to the receiver to eavesdrop on the conversation.

"Serena, you can hang up now," Uncle Peter said.

Dang, she thought. How did he know?

Reluctantly, Serena hung up the phone.

19

Serena's dreams were awful Wednesday night, and she woke up exhausted, again. Worse, Henry was being more of a pain in the butt than ever because he was still mad at Serena for screaming at him, so he'd been dragging his feet all morning long. Which meant that Serena arrived fifteen minutes late to her first-period class and missed a pop quiz. She had to beg her teacher to allow her to take the quiz after school, taking an automatic five-point deduction and making her late for rehearsal.

Rehearsal was awful, too. Mr. Hobbs nitpicked everything she said or sang, making her more flustered than ever before. She actually sang off-key two or three times. Off-key! Her! By the end of rehearsal she wanted to cry. And when it started raining during the walk home, that was the final straw. Serena started bawling. Henry walked next to her, saying nothing. He stared ahead gloomily, and Serena noticed that his face looked awfully wet, too—whether from raindrops or tears, she didn't know.

FRIDAY MORNING WAS CLOUDY AND GRAY. TRY AS SHE might, Serena couldn't shake the feeling of doom she'd had since the moment she woke up. A vague feeling of sadness had settled in her chest.

At lunchtime she wanted to go to the office and call her uncle to see if he'd arrived yet, but she knew that if he told her he wasn't coming she'd lose it—go stark raving crazy right there in the office. So instead she grabbed a bunch of food she knew she wouldn't be able to eat and sat at the table watching Kat eat off her tray. She ignored the chatting around her, wondering what her father was doing at that very moment, and why he wasn't back to his normal self yet, despite his trip to the doctor. Weren't doctors and medicine supposed to make you better?

REHEARSAL BROKE UP EARLY THAT AFTERNOON BECAUSE Mr. Hobbs had an interview with the grant committee. Serena was glad. She loved rehearsals, but she'd felt jittery all day long and tired, as usual. All she wanted to do was go home, let Uncle Peter take over dinner and everything else, and see if she could find an old musical to watch on TV. Gathering her things, she looked around for Henry. He was sitting with Elijah, pulling out art materials.

"Come on, Henry, we gotta go," she said, walking over to them.

Henry scowled at her. "I'm staying. We need to make the farmhouse look older."

Serena felt a flash of irritation, but squelched it. She didn't want to holler at him here. She was tempted to tell him that Uncle Peter was coming. She knew that would definitely get him moving. But if he wasn't there, Henry would just nag her to death until he finally showed up, which was why she hadn't told him in the first place.

"Look," she said. "If you think about it, on Monday the farmhouse *will* be older. Come on, dude, let's go home!"

"*Relájate hermosa,*" Elijah said, coming from backstage. "I asked him to stay. I hope you don't mind. There are a few things I want to work on, and straight up, he is my best worker. I'll walk him home."

Serena looked down at Henry, who was busy sprinkling green glitter on a big Oz sign. He ignored her. Elijah was looking at her as if he could tell something else—besides just wanting to get Henry home—was going on. She forced a smile. "Well, okay. As long as you're sure."

"I'm sure," Elijah told her. "Go home and rest." He held her coat so she could get it on. "You look all stressed out today."

"Gee, thanks," she said. "You really know how to make a girl feel good."

"I didn't say ugly, I said stressed out. You're still a hottie."

"Yeah, whatever. So, really, it's okay for him to stay?" Serena glanced down at Henry, who was now totally engrossed in strategically sprinkling glitter.

"Yeah, it's cool," Elijah said. "I do honestly need his help, and he actually works."

So Serena dug in her purse and pulled out a couple of candy bars she'd been saving.

"Don't cause Elijah any problems, 'kay?" she said to Henry. "Here, you can have one now, and the other after you eat dinner. Call home if you need me." Henry took the candy bars, and then looked up at her. Finally, she could see that the anger was melting away. She wished she'd thought of appealing to his sweet tooth sooner.

"Okay, sissy," he said. *"Adios."* Serena laughed and bent to give him a quick kiss on the cheek. He smiled at her and returned to his glitter.

"Thank you, Elijah."

"Um, sure," Elijah said, walking her to the stage steps. "Can I get one of those, too?"

Serena rummaged through her purse. "Oh, I only had two. I have some gum though."

Elijah laughed. *"Tu eres tan bella."*

Serena grinned. "I understood that, sort of."

"Bueno, entonces dáme un beso," Elijah said, leaning closer to her.

"You and that freaking Spanish," Serena replied softly. But she leaned in and did as he'd asked. She gave him a kiss.

SERENA RUSHED HOME BECAUSE SHE WANTED TO EAT, shower, maybe even a take a leisurely bubble bath, before Henry appeared. Uncle Peter would be there soon, which allowed her, for the first time in a long while, to think of stuff that had only to do with her.

Daydreaming about Elijah and the kiss they'd shared, she drifted to her house in a very pleasant daze. But as soon as she stepped inside she knew something wasn't right. She stood at the front door, looking around, trying to put a finger on what had changed. Finally, it dawned on her. The house was spotless. All the surfaces were dusted, the rugs vacuumed, and the wood floors swept and mopped. There were no piles of old newspapers, no stacks of mail. She peeked into the kitchen and saw that there were no dishes on the table or any pots lying in the sink.

"Whoa," she muttered. She looked out of the front window to see if she spotted her uncle's car. She didn't. Serena was about to head upstairs to see if the clean extended there as well, when something on the fireplace mantel caught her eye. An envelope, addressed to her and Henry in her father's artistic handwriting, was leaning up against the photos that had been polished and straightened. With a trembling hand, Serena opened it.

My Dearest Children,
    I love you and I am so sorry.

With a gasp, Serena dropped the letter, ran through the kitchen, yanked open the back door, and sprinted to the garage to look for her father. Both cars were there, empty. She raced back to the house, running so fast she stumbled down the basement stairs, barely catching herself before she fell. He wasn't in his office either. Serena flew upstairs, taking the steps two at a time.

The door to her father's bedroom was ajar. Serena looked in and saw her father putting something in his mouth, then taking a swig from a bottle of vodka he clutched in his hand. With a shriek, she flung the bedroom door open. Her father dropped the bottle and stared at her. Serena noticed a long thin line of white pills on his dresser, their translucent orange bottles lying on the bed beside him, empty.

"What are you doing here?" her father muttered. His words were slurred, barely coherent.

Serena ran at him, full speed, taking him completely by surprise and knocking him off the bed. Sitting on top of him, she pounded on him, hitting as hard as she could.

"How could you! I hate you!" she screamed. "You were really going to do it, weren't you? I hate you!"

"I'm sorry, baby girl," he said. "I'm so, so sorry." He lay crying in loud, gulping sobs, allowing Serena to pound on him.

Finally, exhausted, Serena rolled off him and put her head in her hands and began crying herself.

Her father lurched up and stumbled to the bathroom. He slammed the door shut, and Serena heard him vomiting.

After a minute, he returned, and sat next to her on the floor.

"I guess I thought that this would be best for everyone," he said. "I'm sorry, baby girl. Please forgive me. I shouldn't have done it. I just . . ."

Her father reached out for her. Serena looked at him for a moment, feeling such a wave of anger that her muscles felt frozen. But seconds later, she fell into his arms. They held each other tightly and sobbed.

SERENA WASN'T SURE HOW LONG SHE AND HER FATHER stayed there crying. It seemed that no time had passed at all before she heard the front door open and her uncle Peter's voice calling out, looking for them.

"We're up here, Uncle Peter!" Serena yelled back.

Her uncle Peter appeared at the bedroom door and surveyed the scene. As he took everything in, a look of disbelief quickly replaced the broad smile that had been on his face. Leaving her father's side, Serena went and leaned against him.

"I guess I got here just in time," Uncle Peter said, giving her a tight hug.

"No," Serena said miserably. "You got here too late."

Feeling completely drained, Serena sat on the bed and let her uncle Peter take over.

"We need to get you to a hospital, bro," he told her father, pulling him off the floor. "They might need to pump your stomach. I'll call 9-1-1."

Serena's father nodded slowly and lay down on the bed. His face looked ashen. Uncle Peter snatched up the phone and dialed hurriedly.

After making the call, her uncle Peter pulled Serena into another bear hug.

"I'm so sorry you had to deal with this all alone, Serena," he said, his voice shaking. He swiped a tear away from his cheek. "You tried to tell me but I didn't hear you. I just never thought he would . . . Look, things will be fine. I'll stay with you guys for the next few months. As long as I need to. That way I can make sure my knuckleheaded brother gets the help he needs. Let you go back to being a kid. I'm so sorry, Serena."

Serena gave him a squeeze but said nothing. She couldn't talk.

Uncle Peter hugged her back and whispered, "I need you to do one last thing for me though. Right now."

Serena nodded tiredly even though she didn't think she had it in her to do anything at all.

"You're a superstar, my beautiful niece, with the voice of an angel," Uncle Peter said. "And I need you to sing. Right now. Sing for your dad. Please."

Tears began to pour down Serena's face. "I can't," she whispered, shaking her head.

"Yes, you can, sweetie," Uncle Peter said gently. "Your dad needs it. I need it." He paused and glanced over at her father before looking down into her eyes. "You need it, too."

Serena closed her eyes and ignored the warm tears that were coursing down her cheeks. Instead, she focused on trying to picture the last scene in the play. She imagined herself in the middle of the stage. She thought about the part of the song when the Scarecrow, the Tin Man, and the Cowardly Lion slowly began to walk backwards off the stage, leaving her standing alone, center stage, as her character left Oz to return home.

"Sing, honey," Uncle Peter whispered.

And, as she began to hear the blare of sirens growing louder in the distance, Serena opened her eyes, took a deep breath, and sang.

Epilogue

Serena paced backstage listening to the first strains of the intro. Out of nowhere, Elijah appeared. He extended his pinkie. She smiled and locked her pinkie with his. "Break a leg, Serena Star," he whispered. Then he leaned over and gave her a kiss.

"Thank you," she whispered. "For everything."

Ever since that terrible Friday in February, Elijah had had her back. He'd come over for dinner the next night and when Henry had fallen asleep and Uncle Peter left them alone to watch a movie, Serena had told him everything. She hadn't felt embarrassed. Instead, it was as if a great weight had been lifted off her heart—like she wouldn't have to face problems all alone anymore.

As for the hundreds of favors, well, Elijah refused to collect on any of them. Every time she tried to repay him he just laughed and said he liked her owing him. She whined and protested, but deep down she knew that she could never pay back all the kindness and support he'd shown her.

"Knock them dead!" Elijah kissed her again and faded into the darkness.

The overture started to fade as the curtain went up. Peeking through a break in the curtain, Serena could see Uncle Peter and next to him Henry, his face aglow even in the darkness of the auditorium. Kat sat behind Henry. She leaned forward and whispered something in his ear that made him smile. Her father was there, too. He had his camcorder pointed steadily at the stage and a huge smile of pride on his face. Already he was starting to look healthier. More himself. Serena knew he had a long way to go before he could shake himself free of the blue completely, but they were beginning to feel like a real family again, and that was a good start.

As the sixth grader who played Toto scurried onto the stage, Serena caught a glimpse of Elijah sliding into the empty seat next to Henry, who sat whispering into Uncle Peter's ear, pointing at the scenery. Everyone who truly mattered to her was right there—front row center, supporting her.

"Toto!" Serena yelled out from behind the curtain. "Toto, you come back here!"

Then, taking a deep breath, she ran onto the stage, into the bright spotlight.

GOFISH

TRACI L. JONES

What did you want to be when you grew up?
A copywriter at an advertising agency. When I was growing up, there were a lot of commercial jingles. I loved them and I wanted to write them.

What's your favorite childhood memory?
I love my childhood memories of holidays. Christmas, Halloween, Thanksgiving, Easter. My mother had a way of making them special.

What were your worst subjects in school?
Science and math. They are so absolute. No room to wiggle or imagine. 2 + 2 is always, always 4. I just didn't like it, and therefore, never put forth a great deal of effort.

What was your best subject in school?
English!

What was your first job?

I got my very first job when I was in eighth grade. My closest friends and I worked as "set-up" girls at a restaurant after school. We'd replace candles, fold napkins, and set the tables before it opened. The pay was pretty bad, but we got as much free pop as we wanted, and enough money to buy a lot of lip smackers lip gloss and Love's Baby Soft perfume.

How did you celebrate publishing your first book?

I was actually on the way to celebrate a friend's birthday when I found out that FSG wanted to publish *Standing Against the Wind*. He was gracious enough to share his birthday celebration with me.

Where do you write your books?

Unlike most writers, I don't have a set time or place to write. Often the best writing I do is while I'm sitting in my car, or outside of a gym, waiting for my kids' soccer or basketball practice to end.

Where do you find inspiration for your writing?

So far, all my ideas from books come from their titles. I can't start writing a book, until I know what its going to be called. For me, the title is the foundation, the framework from which I build a story. I get my titles from everywhere. I love words, and I'll hear a phrase that captures my attention, and the next thing I know I have an idea for a story. For *Silhouetted by the Blue*, that phrase comes from one of my favorite songs, in one of my favorite Broadway plays, *Ragtime*.

Which of your characters is most like you?

I invest many of my characters with little parts of me; in *Standing Against the Wind,* Patrice's shyness is from me, in *Finding My Place,* Tiphanie's background is similar to mine, and in *Silhouetted by the Blue,* Serena's love of musicals is from me.

What sparked your imagination for *Silhouetted by the Blue*?

I've always been a musical theater fan. The first album (yes, record album because I'm that old!) I brought was *The Sound of Music,* and every Saturday I would curl up in my bed and watch the old MGM musicals that came on PBS. Fast-forward to adulthood, and my love for people singing and dancing as a way of moving the story forward hasn't changed. My favorite musical is *Ragtime,* and has been since I first saw it. There is a lovely song in the beginning of the second act where two adult characters are watching their children play along the Jersey Shore near the turn of the century. It is a short, beautiful duet, with heartbreakingly beautiful melodies, and my favorite lines are "Two small lives, silhouetted by the blue, one like me and one like you."

Well, I was singing along with it one day in my car and I was, as always, struck by the beauty of the cadence and image of the words "silhouetted by the blue." I thought to myself, I want to write a story called *Silhouetted by the Blue.*

Why did you decide to deal with the issue of depression in the book?

Once I decided that *Silhouetted by the Blue* was going to be my title, I needed a story line and characters to flesh it out. I find it very difficult to write if I don't have a title, which, I have found, is backward from many other writers. From the start, it was the word "blue" that I focused on. Blue is a color, but more interestingly, blue is also a way of saying you feel sad or depressed. Living with depression was the idea that fired me up. Then it occurred to me that "silhouette" means the shape or outline of something, so what if the character was the silhouette and her life was being shaped or outlined by the depression, or the blue, of someone close?

What do you hope readers will take away from *Silhouetted by the Blue*?

In a single word: hope. Kids have always dealt with very serious life issues, and that is why my books tend to be realistic fiction, rather than science fiction or fantasy. I want to write books where a reader can recognize a problem they or their friends may be dealing with and see what mistakes and choices a characters makes when confronting situations that occur in real life. In the end, I want them to feel uplifted, and most importantly, I want them to have a feeling of optimism about the world around them. I deeply want them to come away from my books feeling that even with serious problems in their lives, with strength (and maybe a good friend), they can get through anything.

When you finish a book, who reads it first?
My writing group, Helen, Jackie and Lisa, get to read the book as it unfolds, a chapter or two each month. Once a book is finished I don't really show anyone but my FSG editor. My family is so supportive they'd love anything I wrote, whether it was any good or not, so they aren't objective and have to wait till it is published to read it! I really rely on my writing group to keep the book, and me, on track throughout the writing process. They've not steered me wrong yet!

What's your idea of the best meal ever?
One that someone else cooks, while I talk to my family and friends at the table.

What time of year do you like best?
I love summer. I like warmth and sun and green and blooming plants. I love warm mornings and warm evenings after long sunny days. I was born in August, so maybe that's why I like summer so much.

What is your worst habit?
I love computer games. I'll get addicted to one and will try and top my last best score and then next thing I know, an hour has gone by.

What would readers be most surprised to learn about you?
I entered college as a English major, which isn't surprising. However, in my very first English class, Shakespeare, I

was told repeatedly by my professor how awful my writing was. After each paper, I'd receive a page full of criticisms from the professor. It took one semester, and one person, to undo years of confidence instilled in me from the positive reinforcement I received from countless elementary, junior, and high school teachers. Looking back, it's amazing how easy it is to believe the negative over the positive, with regards to one's abilities.

By the end of my freshman year, I was a Psychology major, I'd stopped reading for pleasure, and I didn't take another English class again until the last semester of my senior year. That class was a creative writing class and it re-ignited my love for books and for writing.

What is your favorite fictional character?
That is such a hard question. If I had to pick, I'd have to choose the ones I find the most memorable and the ones that were most fun to read. So, I guess if forced I'd go with Fred and George Weasley, and Bud from *Bud, Not Buddy*. I think these characters are vividly written, really memorable, and fun to read.

Patrice Williams is well on her way to get a scholarship to the prestigious Dogwood Academy—despite her absent mother and misfit status at school—until she finds out she needs to get her application signed by her mom . . . who's in jail.

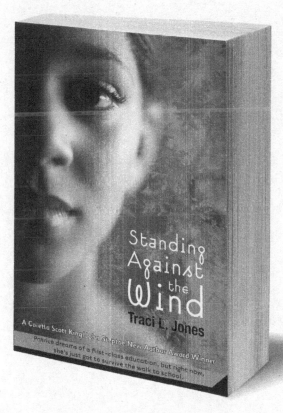

Standing
Against
the
Wind
Traci L. Jones

A Coretta Scott King/John Steptoe New Author Award Winner
Patrice dreams of a first-class education, but right now,
she's just got to survive the walk to school.

Read on to find out how Patrice overcomes every obstacle to get to her dream school.

1

MOST DAYS, Patrice Williams really didn't know which she liked least: walking home or actually getting there.

"Just two more blocks," she whispered to herself as she stood waiting for the light.

During the bitterly cold days of winter, the thirteen-year-old had gotten into the habit of counting the blocks until she was safe at home—safe from the freezing cold wind, safe from the nasty comments made by girls who had cut school and were always hanging out in front of the local drugstore, safe from the gang of boys who had all but quit school and who hung out in the broken-down playground in front of her building. They all seemed to have something mean to say about her.

"One more block."

Patrice's quick steps slowed as she noticed the gang of boys from her middle school gathered at the foot of the stairs in front of her building. She had hoped that Chicago's frigid cold would have driven them inside. But even in this weather they were assembled at the only unlocked entrance, attempting to make everyone else's life miserable. They were talking and laughing, looking like teen dragons as the puffs of warm air from their mouths mixed with the clouds of cigarette smoke they blew nonchalantly. Those not smoking blew on their hands and rocked back and forth on their feet, trying to keep warm and look cool at the same time.

The January wind blew directly into Patrice's face. It seemed to reach right through her coat's thin fabric and under her hand-me-down sweatshirt, and pinch her arms with icy, sharp fingers. With the straps of her old backpack long since broken, Patrice's hand felt frozen in a tight fist around its tattered handle. She shivered again, this time more from nervous anticipation than cold.

Trying not to look at the gang of boys, she stopped at the corner to switch the backpack to the other hand. For a brief moment, she wished she had not given her new Christmas gloves to her little cousin. Her old gloves, so worn that the tips of her fingers were poking through holes, were no match against the weather. Clutching her backpack, she scrunched down deeper into her coat to protect her neck from the cold and crossed the street. She shivered again. No matter which direction she walked in, it seemed that the wind blew right in her face, as if to stop her from moving forward.

Patrice was always cold. Her grandmother would have said it was because she was too thin, not enough meat on her bones. Patrice's grandmother used to try and fatten her up with an endless parade of after-school cakes, cookies, and pies.

"Some chocolate cake for my cocoa grandbaby," Grandma would say as she slid an oversized plate of sweets in front of her. And maybe if she had stayed with her paternal grandmother, Patrice wouldn't be a walking stick. But since her mother had spirited her away from her grandmother a little over a year before, her small frame looked as if it hadn't gained one ounce. There was nothing big about Patrice except her large doelike brown eyes and her famous mop of hair.

The only reason Patrice was noticed at Martin Luther King, Jr. Middle School, and in her new neighborhood, was her abundant hair. So aggressive was it that it almost seemed alive. With effort, it could be coaxed into thick braids and ponytails, or even reluctantly convinced to lie in thick, shiny waves that tickled her shoulders. But since there was no one, including Patrice herself, with the time or motivation to coerce her hair into a style, it was usually a big poof that threatened to swallow her head whole. One of her eighth-grade classmates told Patrice that her hair had all the personality, leaving none for the shy, studious girl who lived underneath it.

As she got closer to the building, Patrice quickly surveyed the group, looking for the only semi-friendly face she could hope to find. She breathed a tiny sigh of relief when she saw Monty Freeman. While Monty wasn't her friend, she knew he wouldn't let the other boys harass her too much. She didn't know what made him cut off their teasing—he never even talked to her—but she was definitely grateful for his sympathy.

Of the five or six boys, there were only three who ever caught her attention. Monty she liked, because of the pity he took on her; Eddie Brooks and Rasheed Walters she despised. They seemed to take pleasure in making her miserable.

Throwing her shoulders back and pretending to be braver than she felt, Patrice picked up her pace and marched toward the steps. She flashed a brief, shy smile at Monty, who returned her acknowledgment with the tiniest, quickest, and, of course, coolest lift of his chin. The other boys smirked at one another and sauntered to the center of the steps, creating a barrier, blocking her access to the door.

"Hey, Puffy!" sneered Eddie. "When you gonna get that hair of yours done?"

Monty shot a quick neutral glance at Eddie. The other boys snickered, and Patrice's shoulders dropped a bit.

"Yeah, Puffy!" added Rasheed. "Them naps on your head are bad. Ain't your sister still working over at the Cut'n'Style? You need to ask for a family discount."

"Shoot, if her sister is still at the Cut'n'Style, I'll go there myself. She is *too* fine!" hooted Eddie. "Your sister looks good, Puffy. You sure you all got the same mama?"

Patrice threw an angry glare in Eddie's direction and tried to weave her way through the hooting and howling boys, without much success. She didn't know what it was about her that they hated so much, but from the moment she had arrived to live with her aunt they seemed to relish teasing her to tears.

"Leave her alone, fellas," muttered Monty. "As nappy as y'all's heads look, you shouldn't be talking. Let her in."

Heeding their leader's command, the gang of boys cleared a path. Patrice hurried up the stairs and yanked open the door to the building. As it closed slowly behind her, she heard Eddie shout one last nasty comment: "Maybe when your mama get out of jail, she'll comb that head!"

Patrice jabbed the elevator button over and over again, until, through the tears in her eyes, she noticed the OUT OF ORDER sign taped to the door.

With a little whimper, she pulled the stairwell door

open and started up the fifteen flights to her auntie's apartment. At least she would get a chance to stop the tears.

Although the stairwell wasn't exactly what you would call warm, it was better than outside, and the hike up the stairs began to thaw her out. Stopping at the tenth-floor landing, Patrice sat down and tried to compose herself. She knew her auntie Mae would be upset if she came home crying again. Last week she had overheard her aunt talking about her on the phone and it had scared her.

"Yeah, girl, Patrice is a good kid, but she's so tender-hearted. Soft, you know," Auntie Mae had said between puffs on her cigarette. "She smart as a whip in school, but she ain't got *no* street sense. It's hard to believe she's NaNa's daughter. NaNa always had some angle. NaNa's street through and through. Shoot, that's why her fast behind is locked up. But Patrice, she ain't like no kid of mine, or them other kids of NaNa's. Growing up down South with her daddy's mama made her too soft. I don't know if she can make it here or not. Always coming home crying 'bout what them ghetto children be saying to her. When she first got here, they teased her about her accent. Then once she somehow got rid of most of that, it was her hair."

Patrice knew her auntie was right. When she had just arrived, all the kids laughed and mimicked her soft Georgia drawl. Before long she stopped talking to most people, and when she did talk, she tried hard to suppress her accent. She was a shy girl anyway, and the teasing had made her feel worse. Now, even though much of her accent had disappeared, except when she was angry, Patrice was still quiet as a church mouse and twice as shy.

Between puffs on her Newports, her auntie had continued: "Patrice's gotten so quiet. She don't even say nothing back. Just stands there, all hurt. I worry to death about that girl. She may not be able to live here too long. Girl, she can't take it. She ain't got no fight in her. She didn't have much when she got here. Now there ain't no spunk or fire in her at all. This place gonna eat her up. She do help around the house a lot, though. I'll give her that especially since I had to take on that extra job. I get home and can put my feet up 'cause she done done most of my chores. I'll tell you what, though, my sister was right to take that child to her daddy's mama when she was a baby. Miss Shanice Renée Brown did Patrice a disservice by bringing her up here. She's a sweet girl; I hope she can stay that way."

Patrice shook the memory out of her head and stood up. Auntie Mae was the only one of her mother's five brothers and sisters who'd agreed to take her in, along with her older sister, after her mom got sent to Mount Rose Women's Correctional Center. Her fifteen-year-old half brother, Marquis, had been sentenced to a few years at a juvenile boot camp for trying to rob the local grocery store with a BB gun, so he had a place to stay, at least for the next three years. Patrice and her then seventeen-year-old half sister, Cherise, had almost become wards of the state. So the last thing Patrice wanted to do was make her auntie worry. She might say Patrice was too much trouble to take care of. Auntie Mae worked two jobs and was always so tired. Patrice felt like a burden and went out of her way to help.

She used her still unthawed hands to wipe any trace of tears from her face. Gathering her stuff, she finished hiking the rest of the way to apartment 1525.

Even before opening the door, she could hear the yells coming from inside the apartment.

"It's *my* turn to pick the show!" shouted Nefrititi, Auntie Mae's seven-year-old daughter.

"Is not!" retorted MarcAnthony, her nine-year-old brother. "You were watching that stupid rabbit show when I got home!"

"Hey, guys," Patrice greeted them. "What's the problem now?"

"MarcAnthony won't let me watch my share of TV," whined Nefrititi. "He got to watch two shows yesterday. I should get to watch two shows today."

"Yesterday's all done. Today's a new day!" Marc-Anthony boomed in a deep voice, imitating the preacher at their church.

"Is your homework finished? What about your chores?" asked Patrice, moving the day-old newspapers, half-empty glasses, and overfull ashtrays off the wobbly dining room table and pulling out her schoolwork.

"Yeah," replied MarcAnthony. "It's right there. Mom helped me today." With one hand, he gestured to a pile of paper hanging over the edge of the table, and with the other, he fended off his little sister.

Some cigarette ashes had spilled onto his homework, and he had put a half-empty glass of milk on it as well, leaving a damp circle over problems six and seven. His other schoolwork lay on the floor, scattered under the table. But, despite the mess, the homework was indeed finished.

Patrice sighed. "MarcAnthony, how many times do I have to tell you to put your homework in your backpack when you're done. Where's Auntie Mae? Didn't she walk you home today?"

"Yeah. She just went to the store to get some more cigarettes. Plus, she gotta send a money order to your mama."

Patrice frowned. Mama oughta be sending money to Auntie Mae, not the other way around. Auntie Mae had enough trouble making ends meet since they cut her hours at the factory.

"Why you frowning, Puffy?" asked Nefrititi. "What you mad at?"

"I'm not mad at anything," snapped Patrice. "And stop calling me Puffy. My name is Patrice."

"I know, but everybody at your school calls you Puffy, and them boys downstairs call you Puffy, and your hair's all puffy," Nefrititi rattled off.

"Yeah, so what," Patrice spat. "If everyone jumped out the window, would you be dumb enough to jump, too?"

"I'm sorry." Nefrititi sniffed, apparently contrite. "Don't be mad. I won't ever, ever call you that again. Okay?"

Nefrititi wrapped her skinny arms around Patrice.

"Okay, okay," Patrice said, freeing herself from the too-tight hug. "I'm sorry I snapped at you. I just don't like being called that."

"Then why you let them do it?" asked Nefrititi, putting her little hands on her hips. "I wouldn't let no one call me some stupid name if I didn't like it."

Patrice looked down at her shoes, unwilling to meet her cousin's defiant eyes, and shrugged. "Just don't you call me that, okay?" she muttered.

MarcAnthony, who had been crawling around the floor gathering his homework during this exchange, stood up and looked at Patrice closely. "Well, your hair *is* puffy, but the rest of you is skinny," he observed wisely. "But since you always help me with my homework and stuff, I won't call you Puffy neither. And I'll knock anybody in the head who does, as long as they're not bigger than me."

Patrice smiled, embarrassed that her young cousins had much more nerve than she did. "That won't be necessary, but thank you for the offer, MarcAnthony."

After getting the TV feud settled and cleaning off the dining room table, Patrice sat down and worked diligently on her homework. Unlike other kids in the eighth grade, she liked homework. Since she didn't have any friends, it didn't cut into her social life, and it gave her something to do besides her chores and taking care of MarcAnthony and Nefrititi. She also liked knowing that she had the best grades in class. No matter what the other kids said or what names they called her, they couldn't take that away.

"Aw, man," whined MarcAnthony, looking around the living room for the remote he had hidden from Nefrititi.

"What's the matter now?" asked Patrice, leaning back in her chair to see if the cable had gone out again.

"My show ain't going to be on," he answered. "Some news stuff is on instead."

Patrice shrugged and turned to finish what was left of her homework when she heard the announcer say something that interested her: "*Scholarships are available for outstanding African American students. Dogwood Academy is one of the five predominantly African American boarding schools in the nation. For more—*"

MarcAnthony had dug the remote out of the sofa and clicked off the TV.

"Wait!" shouted Patrice.

"What?" MarcAnthony said.

"That show, turn it back on!"

". . . and they will send you information about this unique academic opportunity for promising African American scholars, aged thirteen to fifteen."

"Darn it!" shouted Patrice. "What show was that?"

MarcAnthony shrugged. "I don't know. It wasn't *Dragon Ball Z*, though."

Patrice didn't know why, but what little she had heard sent sparks shooting through her body. Staring at the blank television, she made a mental note to be sure to get home quicker tomorrow and watch whichever channel it was until she heard that information again. What she had heard sounded, to her, just like hope.